INTERNATIONAL PRAISE FOR *IN YOUR HANDS*

"A novel about love and loneliness, suffused with a delicate melancholy."
—*Madame* (Germany)

"An extraordinary novel . . . The story, which unfolds with an enviable directness and which garnered the Prémio Máxima de Literatura, follows the lives of three generations: an old woman, her daughter, and her granddaughter. The eldest woman expresses herself by means of a diary; the second (who is a photographer), through commentaries on 10 photographs; and the youngest, in as many letters.

Jenny was married in the 1930s to a homosexual, António, and, in a society based on keeping up appearances, ended up living with him and his lover, Pedro. The latter had a daughter outside of their triangular relationship, Camila, who is, meanwhile, raised by the trio. This daughter experiences intensely all the possible byways of the radical '60s, and, from her relationship with a guerrilla fighter from Mozambique, Natália is born, the letter-writer who narrates the third part of the novel.

At first, you might think that each protagonist is an archetype of her epoch, the dictator Salazar's fascism, the counterculture of the '60s, and the resulting hangover of the aseptic times that followed. But that's precisely where Pedrosa exercises her kaleidoscopic magic: by gathering the scraps of life and narrative, she stirs her protagonists into history and shows how Jenny turns out to be much more transgressive than her liberated daughter or grandchild. Throughout, the three protagonists are driven headlong by their passions and the anarchy of their desires . . . Pedrosa dismantles the conventions of a world configured in the masculine mode."

—*O Globo* (Brazil)

In
Your
Hands

In Your Hands

INÊS PEDROSA

Translated by Andrea Rosenberg

amazon crossing

Previously published as *Nas Tuas Mãos* in Portugal by Dom Quixote in 1997. Translated from Portuguese by Andrea Rosenberg. First published in English by AmazonCrossing in 2018.

"A Poem in Three Parts" from SELF-PORTRAIT IN A CONVEX MIRROR by John Ashbery, copyright © 1972, 1973, 1974, 1975 by John Ashbery. Used by permission of Viking Books, an imprint of Penguin Publishing Group, a division of Penguin Random House LLC. All rights reserved.

Excerpt from *Para Sempre* by Vergílio Ferreira, copyright 1983, reprinted by permission of Quetzal Editores. Translated by Andrea Rosenberg.

Excerpt from *Estórias Abensonhadas* by Mia Couto, copyright 1994, reprinted by permission of the author. Translated by Andrea Rosenberg.

Excerpt from *Fires* by Marguerite Yourcenar, translated by Dori Katz. Translation copyright © 1981 by Farrar, Straus & Giroux. Reprinted by permission of Farrar, Straus & Giroux.

Published by AmazonCrossing, Seattle

www.apub.com

Amazon, the Amazon logo, and AmazonCrossing are trademarks of Amazon.com, Inc., or its affiliates.

ISBN-13: 9781503903258 (hardcover)
ISBN-10: 1503903257 (hardcover)
ISBN-13: 9781503901933 (paperback)
ISBN-10: 1503901939 (paperback)

Cover design by Shasti O'Leary Soudant

Printed in the United States of America

First Edition

In Your Hands

Jenny's Diary

"Who goes to bed with what
Is unimportant. Feelings are important.
Mostly I think of feelings, they fill up my life
Like the wind, like tumbling clouds
In a sky full of clouds, clouds upon clouds."

—*John Ashbery*

1

Your head turned in the direction of my face, your eyes closed, and your mouth moved toward mine on a slow arc of light, laughter, and tears. When your teeth nibbled my lips, someone shouted "Bravo!" the way they do at the opera, and I knew that no girl had ever been loved so much. "Wait," you said, "with us it has to be different." You made my whole body electric with a kiss on the palm of my hand, my giddy fingers stroked the deep curves of your eyelids, and from the soft shock of your hair, I invented a man I could dream of till the glorious day of our ever after. António. I give thee this ring as a symbol of my love and faithfulness.

"António. Pleasure to meet you. My name is António José Castro Morais, but everybody calls me Tó Zé." It was on the third day that you snared me: "Jennifer. Tell your mother you're too tired for a walk today, and come out with me to see what real life is like." My name is Jenny; the father I never actually met admired the heroine of Júlio Dinis's novel *An English Family*—a family quite like our own, actually, in its discreet veneration of wealth as the physical analog to spiritual vigor. But you, António, preferred otherwise. I reinstated your given name, couldn't bring myself to use that banal nickname that made you like everybody else, and you created one for me from the book of my origins. Back then, I thought these contrary efforts were actually identical, an automatic secret code that was clear evidence of love. Only on our wedding night did I discover that there was someone else who called you António, darling. My darling. Watch out. The sun has reached its zenith, and the mountain's every form surrenders to the totalitarian weight of its light. You're walking along, binoculars pointing off at the farthest peaks, and suddenly I see your foot poised in the air, hovering over the precipice. I shout, "Watch out!" and fling my arms around you from behind, and you fall on top of me up in the heights of Meteora. You put an arm around my waist, and your face, jagged in the back-light, cleaves me with the unbearable beauty of a vision. "What's your name, guardian angel?" It was the only time you spoke to me with such familiarity, using the informal *tu*.

You joined us for the rest of our trip in that summer of 1935. You were coming from the monasteries of Mount Athos, where not even the shadow of a woman may enter, and we were coming from the disappointment of Athens, which my mother insisted on describing as "the merry widow of the gods" to show that she was well educated, caustic, and very much a widow. I don't remember the virile statues in the museums of Thessaloniki, only blotches of marble across which your long fingers trailed, almost wanton in the translucency of their bones and fingernails. My fascination with your fingers cost me half a dozen backgammon victories on that day you sneaked me out to see real life in the sumptuous shadows of the Orthodox churches and in wharfside taverns frequented by weathered Greek sailors with Muslim features. You explained the rules of the game, but I was unable to listen, spellbound by your voice, the rapidity of your speech, the mutable color of your eyes—light green when you smiled and then shifting to brown—your sharp nose, perfect and immovable as a decision, your large mouth, thick lips with the corners turned down in a permanently dubious frown.

I was never the talkative sort. My mother reinforced my reticence by teaching me the law of verbal economy: one idea, half a word. I tried desperately to follow your fingers as they moved over the wooden pieces so you'd think me intelligent, capable of beating you. I would never defeat you again.

They say love is born of a combination of buried interests, echoing voices, habits held over from childhood like a wordless melody, passions trampled into the deep mass of time, but in those interwar years nobody was interested in hearing emotions explained in such a manner. Love back then was a formidable product of tedium and innocence, inspired by the carnal aspect of beauty, cruelly magnificent. I loved you suddenly, with a luminous injustice that divided me from all those men who loved me for their similarity to me. They loved me even more afterward, during our long engagement, which made me mundane, and they adored me from the day you officially made me your wife. I'd hear them whispering: *It's strange, she's more like a little girl every day, I never saw anything like it.*

We fell in love at galas and receptions. I gave you my hand, and then Pedro held my other hand, and I felt envy spreading through the ballrooms like a sensual perfume—the two most eligible young men in all of Lisbon were mine. Maybe you weren't even particularly handsome. When I look back at the photos now, in tranquil reminiscence, I see two dapper youths attempting through the distinctiveness of their dress—broad-brimmed hats, patterned silk foulards, Italian waistcoats, wide-shouldered jackets—to minimize certain irregularities of forms and features. You were thin, the two of you, Pedro slightly taller and almost gaunt.

You went everywhere together, and your eyes never lingered on a woman. You talked of painting, literature, travel; you despised politics and business. The combination of those interests, so unusual in men at the time, and your casual indifference to the affectations of feminine beauty made you irresistible. Your entrance would elicit a smoldering murmur, the young women clutching each other's wrists and whispering, "Look who's here, the sun and the moon." You, my dear António, were the intriguing moon, despite your blond hair and your substantially more decisive bearing than Pedro's. He was the dark-haired sun, dazzling with his eternal smile. There was also a sort of splendor swirling around the pair of you that dimmed when one of you appeared without the other.

For me, António, you scintillated in your own way; you radiated a cloudy, purplish light that shook me like a rush of fever. I followed your steps mechanically when we danced, without hearing the music. I would nearly swoon with embarrassment and pleasure at hearing the thrumming of blood, thundering, hypnotic—I never knew whether it was from your heart or mine. No one had ever seen you dance before.

The girls swarmed around me, asking what witchcraft I'd worked on you. The boldest among them, I was told, had attempted numerous times to twirl around in your arms or Pedro's, but in vain. I grew weary of girl talk; I never had a best friend. I found such complicity disconcerting—I knew them too well from school, to which my mother had packed me off for five years to be "formed and disciplined" in the English manner she'd inherited from her parents.

I think I never got over the way, there in the dining hall before the morning recitation of the paternoster, Vera giggled as she described an erotic dream featuring Salazar, Portugal's dictator at the time, and exclaimed, "Girls, I think I need to find myself a husband." Almost all of them received love letters signed with female names—"Beloved friend, look up at the moon tonight at nine thirty, and I will be looking at it too. Missing you desperately, Alexandra"—and the nuns, who read everything, didn't find it odd that girls should write to each other so rapturously; it didn't occur to them that it was the boys from the military academy writing those letters signed by Alexandras and Paulas and Júlias.

Uniforms—people fell for each other over the forbidden thrill of uniforms. I had a dead father, one who died with a chest full of military medals without my ever seeing him, in 1917, in service of the future of a Europe that did not yet exist. You wore white linen or gray flannel, and almost always, rather than neckties, silk scarves, which made me dizzy, hungry for your long, boyish neck.

Nobody really knew what you did for a living—you traveled a lot, for business, you would say, and quickly change the subject. My mother was dazzled by what she called modesty; a beau who showed up with a chaperone in tow and didn't boast of his professional status was a miraculous find. "I have no idea what such an *exquisite* young man ever saw in you," she told me once, in the playful tone she used to express the most heartfelt truths. She always found a way to include one or two English words in every sentence, and *exquisite* was one of her favorites. On our wedding day, she switched to addressing you with the informal *tu* and gave you a motherly hug. She asked if you were really prepared to make "this little lady" happy, and you answered her in German. Had I done such a thing, she would have called me impertinent and pouted in humiliation.

My fragile mother would never admit to being supplanted by unfamiliar knowledge, so she always considered me to be a step behind her. "Give that here, I'll do it, you won't be able." I heard that old refrain repeated every time I attempted anything new; it was almost despite her that I learned to play the piano—"Get away from there, child, you're just putting the piano out of tune. You think passion can make up for lack of skill." For her, passion was something only creators had. We'd already been married several months when you said, "You are so marvelously intense, Jennifer. I never thought a woman could be so intense." That was perhaps the highest praise you ever gave me, and the hostilities between me and my mother ended right there and then. My passion, it turned out, was a gift, a virtue that had led you to choose me to be the only woman in your life, the bearer of your name, mistress of all that was yours.

Pedro enjoyed slowly brushing my hair and then plaiting it; you always liked seeing me in braids and ribbons. During Pedro's numerous trips away, I would shorten the hemlines of my delicately embroidered white dresses, put on bobby socks, and nestle in your lap while you stroked my face, my hands, my legs. Once you even laid me down on the ground and covered my chest with tender bites and soaked it with tears; you were on the verge of taking me, and then you begged for my forgiveness. I told you, "Come on and enter me, don't be afraid," and you said, "I can't, my angel. It wouldn't be fair to you. I belong to him, Jennifer. If you want to leave me, you should."

Leaving is not an act of will but a consequence of forgetting, my love. If you'd loved another woman, my wounded pride would have found the strength to dump shovelfuls of earth into the dark pit of my chest. But your forbidden love pushed you into that tragic limbo where my love for you was doomed to reside. Not for a second did I consider ending our marriage. And yet there was more than just wild passion and boundless understanding in my decision to stay with you. There was also vanity, my dear António. I couldn't have borne my mother's dismal scorn or the laughter of gossiping girls. In my grief at your disaffection, I was unable to face such torments. Little by little, I managed to gird myself with the elemental joy of being your wife. You, who had no interest in women, had chosen me to be by your side for our whole lives. The sex I'd never had could not rob me of the ecstasy of this adventure. I would remain your beloved, and your lover's accomplice.

Camila says unrequited love is bad for the complexion, deforming the features and turning the skin sallow, but that was never the case with us, António. Lack of requital gave you a golden glow—you were transformed the day Camila arrived. "How could you betray me, Pedro?" You wept in his arms all night, and eventually he persuaded you to accept her, offered her to you while begging your forgiveness and swearing his love to you. And so you gave me a daughter, and she kept me from going mad. During those years in which love was concentrated entirely in fierce physical attraction, a person could live a life just on the taste of another's lips. Or at least I did.

2

Every night of my life I thanked God for the gift of that ever-unchanging emotion. Many marriages collapsed, others swiftly decayed, swept up in the frenetic music of an increasingly troubled era, but ours remained pure, floating above the world's tribulations.

At the end of the reception, the three of us went up the stairs, holding hands, seized by a fit of laughter. "Aren't you going to carry your bride over the threshold?" someone asked, and you answered, "No, she's the one leading us by the hand." The girls let out little shrieks of excitement, called me a lion tamer, and tossed flowers at me. I felt dazed as the petals rained down, the champagne rising to the most lucid corners of my skull, opening all the doors that connect the soul to the entrails. In the dark hallway, the sound of your voice was as clear as a mirror: "Jennifer, darling, sweet girl, you'll sleep in Pedro's room. Go on and see if you want to change anything more to your liking. We want you to feel at home here, my dear." Then you chucked me under the chin, Pedro planted a kiss on my head, and the two of you went into our bedroom, the one with my grandmother's big four-poster bed and the intricately stitched linen bedding that she'd embroidered to celebrate my entrée into the world of real love.

I didn't understand why nothing was happening the way social norms indicated things should, but that night I didn't even feel sad. I was exhausted from smiling and dancing all day, tired of being beautiful and lively in a heavy dress better suited for royalty than for a wedding, and I thought only that you wanted to protect me, as always, or that you were prolonging the perverse pleasure of waiting a little bit longer. Again and again I twisted the wedding ring on my finger, filled its warm gold with kisses, and fell asleep, no longer afraid of that final moment of surrender that had so unsettled my dreams.

I never told anyone this story. It didn't seem to be of any interest—people are bored by happy tales, and with good reason: happiness calls up those parts of us that are most melancholy and lonely. I've started writing it now most of all for Camila—I am afraid that one day she'll discover all the facts and be angry with us. There's no such thing as facts, my dear Camila: they are game pieces we create and move around to make ourselves feel victorious, or at least secure. Everyone has his secret, every love its nontransferable code. You were born of our love, and I owe you an effort to decipher the code that is your inheritance, the light given to you, that you might transform it into your own particular vision.

Above all, do not seek in love a path that is not there. At the end of the war, finding themselves surrounded by ruins, people believed they could save the world through construction. Builders grew wealthy and began to be called contractors and were universally admired. Utility became the predominant value; philosophers studied natural sciences; social anxieties were laid out on tables as had previously happened only with pie crust, live animals, and human cadavers; and private practices were set up to solve people. And love, which has no solution, disappeared.

Time took its place, but time turns in the opposite direction from light, moving from white to black. That's why it has to turn faster and faster, and so life passes by without our noticing. Love, Camila, is the only fetter there is on death—that's what I was tempted to tell you when that bolt of lightning took Eduardo from you. The cruelty of love is precisely that: it fixes life motionless in eternity. But the lightning was exempt because it was so literal. Had it not happened during the day, nobody would have believed that a young man could disappear like that, emerging from the sea, twenty years old, riven by a bolt of lightning plunging from the sky.

Light has its strategies and its chosen few. You were marked by it from birth: without that tongue of fire turning your first beloved to ashes, you might never have found that out. Don't think I'm here to cover over the plot of your existence with gold leaf. No, my only aim is to describe the potential truth of these seventy-five years of mine.

As you know, I never had to look for work or develop a skill. It's agonizing for me sometimes to see you torn apart by money, Camila; you get furious with me, say it's people's subservience that you find so appalling, the ease with which they stoop to power and abandon everything they believe in, but it is money that makes people stoop like that, shiny money that garbs them in the color of time, a long mantle made of rectangular scraps of paper that they mistake for glory and eternal happiness. You swiftly respond that that's the way it's always been, which is probably true, but I'm part of the last generation of women who were spared the indignity of having to earn a living. I saw the Marquise of Faya placing her last chips on the green felt of the gaming table, saw her die at the croupiers' feet and be shoved down the table by the eager feet of other losers, but I never saw two female friends competing for an employer's favor.

Now that the wars are over, the main thing people seem able to survive is themselves, and that's the scariest thing of all.

If only your work didn't so closely resemble love, Camila—but that promiscuity infiltrates you like a disease. You wanted to live off your talent, and now it's grinding you up in its gears. Photographs of an earth without a heaven; however much you talk about the need to be detached and ironic, I can't help seeing a dense haze of ice blurring the lines of your flawless images. You put into your photography a discipline you never find in life; as people hurt you by omission, you shut yourself in your darkroom to fiddle with contrast levels.

Though I endured periods of remarkable upheaval, the steady circumstance of love always remained unchanged at the center of my life. All my life I was as passionate about António as António was about your father, and the two of them loved me—love me—the same way I do, solidly, with mutual understanding. It's hard for me to say "in my time," the way people my age always do, because my time is simply that of sharing love with my loved ones. That's why you, who arrived in my arms six years after my wedding day, are the same age in my heart as your father or his lover, who gave me the great fortune of knowing love. We endure the sharp blade of changeable moods and the slow persistence of interdependencies. You arrived at the right moment, Camila, because being in love closes us off from the world. And prison exacerbates the worst in us, even if we are unaware.

At first their intimacy was hard on me. I spent whole nights with my ear pressed to the wall, hating their mingled voices, the conjoined rhythm of their bodies, the moans and slumber. I was so afraid of the startling things that happened in that room that I stopped sleeping altogether.

I spent days and nights and nights and days in a trance, wandering through a house full of ghosts, singing lullabies about fairies and guardian angels, until I collapsed on the porch, dazed with sun and exhaustion. I would wake up the next morning with their hands stroking my hair, in the large four-poster bed where my mother was born.

"Are you calmer now, silly?" António asked me, and I saw our three naked bodies aglow in the mirror on the dressing table, our legs chastely intertwined as in a children's game.

And for our entire lives we loved each other the way children do, never crossing over into eroticism, in a ruthless make-believe of pleasure and pain.

All there is to know about love is astonished acceptance. A person can't learn to love, Camila; no democratic endeavor can dole out passion in those pockets of poverty where it cannot reach, no factories can mass-produce it for assembly, construction, or export. There is nothing just about this emotion: indeed, justice is merely a performance of putting the world in order, a circus we created to replace the irrational law of the heart.

Do not look for an explanation of my life, and do not view it with sorrow or shock; when I reach my doddering old age, read in these journals that I was happy. Do not worry about how or to what extent, and do not succumb to the temptation to distinguish between love and passion: little by little, I have come to see that those distinctions are traps set so that the wool will fall over our eyes and immortality will elude our grasp. Love, Camila, consists of the divine grace of bringing time to a standstill. And that's all there is to say about it.

3

I could have cast aside the ludicrous circumstance of being a married virgin. But I never wanted to, and nobody knew in any case, and at the time chastity had not yet become a public signal of failure.

I had suitors, of course. I particularly remember Manuel Almada, who was almost pathetically sweet, irresistibly condescending, and aristocratically distracted. He was somewhat morose about his reputation for constantly attempting to seduce new conquests, efforts that caused him more humiliations than they gained him trophies. In his youth, through the first movie stills, he'd fallen in love with people he'd never even met. And that pattern continued for the rest of his life.

I recognized an aspect of myself in the way he, perpetually a tourist, declared that all the love one experiences is actually a degradation of love. To love a woman, he claimed, is, in the end, not to love anybody, because women change every single day. He was right. His love never managed to touch me: the woman he saw in me had nothing to do with me. He was almost ten years younger than I, and I found his youth agonizing. I might have been the only woman in the world who eagerly looked forward to growing older. I was horrified by the idea of looking back on my whole life and seeing only the eternally smooth skin of an object with no past. I loved the imperceptible corrosions of time; maybe for that reason, everybody told me I looked younger every day. My disengagement earned me a reputation for kindness. I was fascinated by the determination people invest in their actions, whether for good or for ill.

I think that's why I've aroused such furious passions; all my senses were caught up in fleeting substances. I enjoyed the play of intensities. I'd be kissing one minute, and the next shooing them out and laughing. I laughed because nothing in this world is all that dire. I laughed because I loved, and loving was enough for me.

I no longer remember what sorrow felt like. One of the advantages of aging is managing to forget those things we do not care to recall. I remember one linguist who complained he was unable to forget any of the twenty-something languages he knew. He said he was going mad, his head crowded with useless information. He felt crammed full of trivialities. I'm certainly not going to say that people draw closer to the essence of life in old age; being old hasn't equipped me any better to find a solution to the problems of the universe. But I think I did become more playful, especially after your death, António. I was always a serious girl, and now I've become a frivolous old woman.

At twenty, I battled my insecurities by employing a rather cruel sense of humor. People always said, "That girl's such a cynic!" and I would joke that cynicism was a sign of intelligence. Now my humor has become kinder, more tactful. At least I hope so. I have no wish to hurt anyone. That became essential for me. People spend half their lives mistreating one another, out of fear and a need for affirmation. It's a pathetic and deeply fruitless activity. I am no longer ashamed of being tender; that's one of the things you stripped from me when you died.

You so disliked displays of affection that I recall every single time I pushed you, unwilling, into one. "Jennifer, darling, you are so patient with my friends," you'd say, for example, when Costa Veleno shattered a bottle of port wine on the corner of the Louis XV desk in the parlor while ranting about what he called Salazar's collusion with the English rabble. I laughed as I swept up the shards of glass, amused. Delfim Costa Veleno—"With two *l*s, Jenny, write it with two *l*s. Remember, the name is Italian in origin; my grandfather was one of the most distinguished members of Victor Emmanuel II's court"—was a devastating spectacle, his blond brow dripping with sweat before the rich and powerful, his short, stout body glittering with energy, his thick lips gleaming indiscreetly between his short goatee and his curly mustache.

Veleno got particularly worked up toward the end of the Portuguese World Exhibition, of which he was, in his words, one of the central pillars. He ranted bitterly about the ingratitude shown by the present toward men who advance "the progress of history," and ended his nights sobbing on the shoulder of his current favorite. These were always beardless youths with the placid and impressionable look of errand boys, whom Veleno wished to transform into well-read dandies. He invariably grew weary of them after a few months, but he didn't give up: he'd switch out one callow young man for another who was just as malleable. Most of them disappeared from our shared lives before we'd even heard the sound of their voices. Once, wild with jealousy, he got in a fight with the poet António Botto in the gazebo in the garden, accusing him of corrupting his disciple.

But our evenings with Veleno always ended early; at a certain point, Delfim would suddenly emerge from the sofa at the rear of the room, still racked with sobs, dragging the boy by the arm, and, rolling his eyes to hide how swollen they were, announcing, "*Bambini*, I'm ravaged to have to deprive you of my company, but I've just remembered that the secretary of foreign trade is supposed to call. And when the nation calls us, we must answer, *Santa Madonna*!"

The secretary never phoned. In the summer of '41, Veleno was drinking apocalyptic amounts, clutching a pamphlet titled *Portugal, Mother of the Future* that had me on the cover. "Look, Jenny. I made a star for them, and they can't even pick up the phone to thank me." As the star he'd made, I attempted to console him and myself with a slow, pious shrug. How you mocked me, António: "From Bohemia's muse to Portugal's mother—that's quite a career path, Jennifer!" If only I'd been able to trigger those passionate storms you reserved for Pedro, my plunge into that greater innocence known as vanity would have been worth it.

Veleno wasn't even around when I was asked to sit for the famous photograph. He insisted on giving us a tour of the marvelous Portuguese World Exhibition, which he considered his—"I want you to know it inside and out, and I want to introduce you to Almada Negreiros, Cottinelli Telmo, and all my other dear artist friends"— but he ditched us as soon as we entered the exhibition grounds in an agitated effort to be seen by Duarte Pacheco and say hello to all the representatives from the diplomatic corps.

I was drinking *capilé* with Josefa Nascimento, one of the few women whose company I enjoyed, in the food tent next to the Catholic Missions Pavilion, surrounded by photographs of African villages full of smiling little black girls, when a gray-haired man with buggy eyes approached and hesitantly addressed me. He told me my face was exactly what he was looking for to go on the cover of a publication about the quintessential Portuguese woman, Eve and the Virgin Mary rolled into one, and he implored me to at least agree to do a few screen tests, even made the additional proposal of a movie role. You and Pedro were leaving the next day for another of your romantic jaunts through the casinos of Portugal and Spain. I accepted immediately, with a swiftness that surprised even Josefa, for whom the world seemed to contain no surprises.

The film turned out to be called *Heaven in Your Eyes*, and the director said that even in black and white you could tell my eyes were green. I still believe they liked my voice, or maybe they simply didn't know how to turn away a young woman so determined to be more than a photograph. In any event, they offered me a radio show responding to mail asking for romantic advice, *Letters from the Heart, by Maria da Felicidade*. It lasted twenty years, and I never told you about it. Not you nor anyone else, not even Camila. As a matter of fact, I suspect that

Camila would look down on me a little if she knew. One day, when I came home from the studio after the program, she told me she'd been listening to this woman Maria da Felicidade on the radio whose voice was just like mine, but more the femme fatale type. She laughed: "As if you were even capable of saying that kind of sentimental claptrap!" I wasn't bad. I projected from my diaphragm and became an expert on men. The program was a way of getting back at you, at the loneliness of my secret, at all the women who didn't have any secrets. It was also, often, a way to keep Rosário on with us after all the other maids had already been let go, or to buy a couple of pounds of meat. *Santa Madonna!* Delfim Veleno never had the pleasure of knowing he was dealing with a radio artist. Two months after the pamphlet came out, he decided I was a lost cause and went back to his usual struggle to clamber up social ladders.

He'd told me his life story as soon as we met. According to him, his father had named him Delfim as a sign that he was destined to greatness, having been born on July 28, 1914, the day the Great War began. His mother died giving birth to him, and his father, in his devastation, became a gloomy bookkeeper who never grew used to that gloom. Delfim had tutors even in his earliest childhood: at four years old he was writing letters and playing the piano. Ambrósio Veleno obsessively exhorted him to genius: the boy had to be a Mozart or a Dante.

One day, in an effort to stimulate his son's aesthetic sensibilities, he pinned a beautiful butterfly to the boy's tie. It struggled frantically there on his chest for what seemed to Delfim, who was seven at the time, an eternity. He sat motionless and mute the whole day, not daring to release the butterfly, silently sobbing. "You're weak," his father told him. "You've got your mother's watery blood." Little Veleno grew up hearing that he was weak, a weak boy who would never be able to fulfill the dreams and glory of the Italian Vellenos. "My father was right—I spent my entire youth being a weakling," he'd sometimes tell his closest friends, gloomily stroking his mouche. "But it wasn't my mother's fault. She came from a very old Jewish family that had passed as converts during the Inquisition, and the Jews are a tough people. They could never give themselves the luxury of frailty, is the thing. The reason Portugal didn't wither away under centuries of constant attacks is because the Jews were bolstering its foundations. As a child, I dreamed every night of my mother's eyes, which had taken leave of me as soon as I was born. Drenched with blood, like a martyr, she sought in me strength I wasn't able to give her. She ended up relinquishing what strength she had to offer it to me. I have been carrying that burden of guilt with me ever since."

Ambrósio Costa Veleno found work as a butler for a noble family so he could send his son to the best school in Lisbon. When the boy turned fifteen, his employers were out of the country, and Ambrósio decided to throw a party in the house and invite Delfim's schoolmates. The party was the talk of the town—so much so that the owners caught wind of it, and Ambrósio lost his job. What happened next goes to show that misfortune can switch on light bulbs similar to those of genius: Ambrósio Veleno went knocking on the door of every business in Lisbon and started a free advertising circular called *The Ad Pages*. The announcements of job openings and houses for sale or rent made the initiative a success. The senior Veleno went from penniless nobility to prosperous bourgeoisie in much less time than it took his son to finish high school. Abundance gradually softened the father's implacable expectations: "Why even bother with business ventures? The longer you stay in school, the more important people you'll meet, and the world's all about networks, not knowledge."

Ambrósio was right. Delfim managed to become vociferously anti-German right before the end of the war and meet a director of the State Defense Police, who set him up with a post in the archives. "Now, with the nation's memory under my care, I can write the novel this century needs," he declared. Josefa Nascimento gave one of her mocking smiles and remarked, "Oh, you poor dear. You think you're as poisonous as if they'd named you Veneno instead of Veleno."

Josefa Nascimento published detective novels under the pseudonym Joseph Birth. "I gave myself an English male name so the books would sell better," she explained to the few in whom she confided her parallel existence. Those obviously did not include Delfim—or Bufo Veneno, Ratfink Poison, as Josefa had so presciently dubbed him. She could spend an entire evening going on about the writer's moral responsibility—with António Botto as a scathing counterbalance, asserting, in his pretentious way, the superior virtue of sensation and the sacred ineffability of the flesh. At a certain point, as Josefa rambled on, he'd yawn ostentatiously and break in: "Cut the speechifying, sweetheart, you're suffocating my soul and making my brain glaze over."

Despite Josefa's moralizing, António Botto was quite fond of her. He liked that she followed her heart even as she volubly defended reason. He was especially moved by the unconditional friendship she offered Judith Teixeira, an audacious poet whose first book—*Decadence*, published in 1923—had been burned by the authorities. Teixeira went on to publish two more books, the second of which, *Naked: Poems of Byzantium*, earned her public opprobrium and drove her into an ever more despondent silence. António Botto shielded her as best he could and used to drag her over to our house in an attempt to cheer her up. Judith's wealth and possessions gradually drained away in her ignominious struggle against time, leaving her practically impoverished. Josefa supported her, with delicacy and constancy, in the last years of her life.

Josefa Nascimento was no beauty. She had close-set eyes above a hooked nose and a scornful mouth, which she made full use of in showing her disdain. But her expansive gestures radiated an enormous calm that defined another kind of beauty. She seemed oblivious to the small injuries of affections, focusing on the gentle saving of the world.

For morality's sake, her father forbade her from going to university; in a fit of rebellion she ended up marrying a lunatic but renowned poet, whereupon responsibility seized her by the throat, forcing her to work and study at the same time. Her nursing degree gave her the necessary knowledge about medicines and doses. She'd become addicted to detective novels as a girl; she'd been an anxious child, and those books reassured her that the power of reason would win out in the end. In her thirties, when she started coming home to an empty house at the end of the workday, she decided to pursue that postponed vocation. She'd never dreamed of writing an autobiographical novel, out of respect for her husband, who, after gambling everything away, ended up in a psychiatric hospital.

"It's really hard to write a good detective novel, which made me think it would be wonderful training for someone who wanted to be a serious writer," she confessed. Later she discovered that she could remain within that genre and still express truths about men, women, and society as a whole. What's more, the noir label brought her a readership, wealth, and impunity: nobody was looking for subversive messages in books titled *In the Darkness of the Heart* or *The Murdered Bride*.

She was most interested, both in books and in life, in exploring the labyrinths of individual choice. I would sidle closer to her as I listened to her talk in a cold, almost inhuman tone about people's compulsions, about good and evil, and about how we choose these words. "In a way I'm very conservative," she'd say, "in the sense that I worry about the rapid changes taking place in things that have already been perfected and worked well for centuries. For instance, I don't like the way we tear down old buildings—on the whole, I think, despite the aesthetic justifications we tender, the buildings we replace them with are even worse. But I'm quite radical in other regards."

She was full of clever revolutionary ideas: she organized teas on the "Joy of Motherhood" where they talked about contraception methods and explained that children's intelligence benefited enormously when their mothers pursued an education and worked outside the home; she created a sort of informal association of female doctors and nurses to tackle women's concrete day-to-day troubles. "In short," she'd say, "I spend my time trying to make the world a little less enervating."

Even as her books started to sell more and more, she never revealed her identity: "You see, Jenny, fame is directly proportional to intrigue. People tend to forget this, terrified of dying unredeemed, and strip themselves bare in pursuit of a bit of celebrity. Also, don't forget that one of the appeals of my beloved Joseph Birth is his sober masculinity. Do you think your friend Veleno would be as enthusiastic about Birth's books if he knew I'd written them?" I laughed. Delfim praised everything embraced by the elite, and Birth was rather fashionable—because he was English, I imagine, and especially because of the unexpected risqué air he acquired from incorporating quotations from D. H. Lawrence and Virginia Woolf into a noir plot. In reality, Veleno had doubtless never read a single page—I found it impossible to believe he could enjoy such virulently feminist mysteries. "Ah," said Josefa, "but nobody would appreciate that feminism, as you call it, if the hand that scribed it were a woman's." She smiled. "Not even women themselves."

In spite of everything, we never grew close. Indeed, I filled the house with friends precisely in an effort to ward off any supposition of intimacy—and especially to shatter the privacy the two of you shared. Or, rather, so that festive crowd of strangers could offer me the illusion of being your wife.

4

You seemed to be made for each other, you and Pedro. A piano and its sheet music. You would have preferred to be the music, but you were forced, by the very excess of your passion, to be merely an instrument that resonated with his melody. I think it was out of love for you that Pedro squelched his own talent. Several talents, in fact: he was an excellent painter, a compelling writer, and he had a magnificent baritone voice. But none of that compared, for him, to the compact perfection of your feelings. He wanted to love you with the obsessive exactitude with which you loved him, and that perpetual gap between impossible desires floated between you like a private sun. Sometimes it was almost hard to see. With his left hand, he would grab the lit cigarette you were holding in your right and start to smoke. Pedro never began anything—he only seized what you'd started in order to slowly finish it.

It was like that from the very beginning. You were playing roulette in Monte Carlo, and you kept losing. A young man with black hair bent over your shoulder and whispered a number in Portuguese. An unlucky number, actually: the day your parents' ship sank on their way to Brazil, where your father owned a coffee plantation. You bet on that number and won. You bet again and again won. At the end of the night, you divided your winnings with the young Portuguese man—Pedro—and ordered him to ditch the whore he had on his arm. Your guardian angel asked that you not use such coarse language, but he obeyed. He kissed the woman's hand, murmured something, and followed you. But the next night you found him in her bed once more. Pedro told you then that that much older woman, the widow of a rich businessman, was the only haven he had. He'd grown up in an orphanage, and from there he'd started working as a warehouse guard in her companies. Eventually she was giving him a monthly stipend to escort her around the world. Then you offered yourself as a substitute for the widow.

Since that summer of 1934, exactly a year before the two of us met in Greece, you and Pedro had become inseparable, or nearly so. Occasionally he slipped through your fingers. You'd wait for him at the doors of cheap hotels. You took that solo trip to Greece to get back at him for one of those waits. Pedro emerged from the hotel with a girl, and you lashed out at him and took off the next day. My love for you was born over the concealed wound of your anger, António. A small betrayal made way for a vast faithfulness.

I never wanted to tell anyone our story, not even Camila or Natália, because even they would feel sorry for me. I wanted them to imagine us as being somewhat debauched, happier. Officially we lived in three separate rooms, and I had the task of stripping what was supposedly Pedro's bed, where in fact nobody slept. It's true that we were happy, since we never formed a conventional love triangle. Most of all, I wanted to keep anyone from guessing at my chastity, which would wrap the three of us in the false mantle of a tragic mistake.

Only after our wedding did I discover the factors that had driven you into my arms in Meteora. Pedro mentioned the trip during an argument with you. The two of you were so worked up that it probably didn't even occur to you that I could hear you in the next room. I wasn't hurt, or even disappointed; I'd gotten used to being a spectator to your raw passion, and I preferred the tranquility of my hopeless, deathless love. I thanked God for the tortuous skill of His writ, which causes wounds to flourish in the most unexpected manners.

With your arrival at this house that had previously been mine, only the view of the Tagus did not change. All I asked of you, António, when you began to transform my gently geometric garden into an imposing, baroque work of art, was that you never cover up that bit of water visible from the bedrooms' balconies, gleaming like a string of diamonds down from the modest houses of Ajuda to the hills on the southern shore. And you complied.

I once saw Pedro down in the garden using shears to cut up a canvas he'd promised to me. You were shaking your head and saying in a choked voice, "Please forgive me. I can't believe I asked you to destroy one of your own paintings. I'm a criminal." In the end he put down the shears, stroked your face, and kissed you on the forehead. You shoved him, told him to go to hell, him and his tenderness, and fled along the lakeshore. He ran after you, pushed you to the ground, flung himself on top of you, and kissed you slowly, violently, on the lips.

The two of you never realized I was up there on the balcony, startled into stillness. I saw everything you could not: the movement of the light in Pedro's black hair, the reflections of the lake pursuing the kisses on your body, a sparrow picking at the painted image of your rumpled clothing. I came to think you were jealous of me. Pedro told me he'd accidentally left the canvas out on the porch one night, and that the cat had scratched it beyond repair. But that same night, in the bedroom, you swore to Pedro you'd never get angry over his work again, said you were going to cure yourself of that awful selfishness, born of your fear of being a failure. "But it was you who created that image, António," he responded. "Don't you remember? It was you who imagined God and the devil seated on the chessboard of the trees in the garden. It was you who dreamed up the garden itself. Sometimes I myself feel like a product of your imagination, and I'm afraid that one day you'll make me disappear."

You used to say that the enormous evergreens, which loomed over us like the shadow of the passing days, were an affront to the precariousness of human existence: "I can bear them only when they've been disciplined, cut back to life's proper proportions." We hired four expert gardeners to create the chessboard that you wanted the garden to become. The hedgerows of boxwood and yew became kings, bishops, pawns, and knights rising fifteen feet tall, and that frenzied effort to bring order created a cushioned atmosphere in which forms seemed to fluctuate like hallucinations. Now tamed, the garden that the two of you had dreamed of making into a work of art became uncontrollable, a labyrinth of hidden vegetal volitions that altered the voice and agitated the instincts of anyone who tarried within it.

With Salazar, whom you so thoroughly despised, you shared a fundamental inability to understand at what point imposing one's will unsettles the serene order of things. You would utter long harangues, proffering reasons as if they were divinely outlined plans. You'd conclude, "It seems to me that this is apparent to any middling intellect," and only Veleno, who was at perpetual risk of becoming supremely middling, would applaud, dazzled. That's why, from the first moment you met at an amateur art exhibition where Pedro was showing a few paintings, Veleno inspired in you a compassion deeper than that found in many relationships. That's why you later defended him, even when his lust for power combined with his cowardice and produced that fateful denunciation.

You used to say that being a person's friend means having the courage to know the best and worst of them, and to store that worst away, however terrible it may be, in the silence of one's heart. Indeed, I've never heard a more precise or poetic definition of friendship. Incredible insight frequently soared through your monologues. And yet those flights almost always led into the impassible mountains of your solitude. You saw any attempt to keep you company as a perverse stratagem for bringing you down.

On one occasion you even stormed out of the room, shaking with fury, just because Josefa pointed out the contradictions in a political stance that you yourself had just criticized. You'd said, "Naturalism is built on acceptance, and we end up trapped in a dictatorship before we realize it. Cosmopolitanism is the only way to avoid that. I'm against nature because it's a right-wing phenomenon: the law of natural selection exterminates the most vulnerable individuals." Josefa broke in to add that, paradoxically, it was the right wing that had stood side by side with the Church to defend the right to life of even the most defective and unviable fetus, and you shuddered, annoyed that you hadn't come up with that logical deduction. Taking advantage of your momentary silence, Josefa said boldly, "I assume, then, that you're also against having sex, which is the means by which nature perpetuates itself. I'm going to start calling you António the angel." "Fine," you said, "since you're not going to let me finish what I was saying, I'm going to bed," and you stalked upstairs without saying goodnight. I laughed. Camila, who was about eighteen by then and just as pigheaded as you, said, "No, don't call after him, Jo. Men always get uncomfortable when women talk about sex and the right to control their own bodies." Pedro said, "Poor child. You don't understand a thing." All too many interesting conversations are ruined that way.

There is, my dear António, a biological brutality to the need to affirm human nature that can destroy the exquisite house of cards of our vast culture in an instant—with just a gentle puff, in a single uneventful evening. Pedro's words expressed his love and guilt toward Camila. But she was deeply wounded by them and many other similar comments, which Pedro, attempting to compensate for an entire lifetime of fakery with a moment of genuine tenderness, made in order to purge her from his blood. The missteps grew like noxious weeds, persistent and imperceptible, causing irremediable hurt.

I believe now that we should have told Camila our secret, which we carried out so poorly. I am certain that our friends, at least Josefa and Manuel Almada, were aware of your love for Pedro, and they loved us, all three of us, all the more for it. However much a scandal seems to go against our values, love makes it dissolve into smoke. The only abomination a person cannot survive is the absence of love, and that was the one we failed to protect her from. What's more, it was a lie: your father loved you very much, Camila, and António was paralyzed with emotion around you because he was deeply in love with your father. That was what we should have told you, not that you were the accidental result of a summer fling and that your father had asked his best friend's wife to raise you. What terrible stories we tell children to disguise the pathetic cast of our own lives. We conceal our true selves and thus maintain the illusion of being in control.

Not even the rubble of two world wars in a single century managed to open our eyes to how laughably little our secrets were worth, António. We didn't dare admit the truth that Camila's birth betrayed. We have no moral ground from which to criticize her generation's morals. We trampled our truest selves in favor of the appearances of power; she tramples on appearances in pursuit of the empowerment of the self. One bit of theater was subbed in for another, and women climbed onstage to replicate that ancient masculine vice of constructing heroes out of mere humans.

To be accepted in the world of men, Camila compartmentalizes herself the way they always did, dividing heart from flesh and thought from emotions; she erects abstract categories like dikes to hold back the molten lava of life. Two equally pathetic and futile efforts. Two eras spinning off track, deafening the absolute voice of chaos with the noisy chatter of reason, that contemporary goddess who finds vengeance for the compartmentalization that gave birth to her in the power of her own discourse.

Natália likes to say I don't have wrinkles because I've had the good fortune to live outside of history—she feels deep resentment for the persistent history that discriminates against her for being the product of miscegenation—and I just give her a smiling kiss so she'll continue to believe she has an old-fashioned grandmother, a sort of steady, portable Christmas season. And at bottom it's true: surrender was my only form of affirmation; I will not die bearing the weight of rusty weapons.

I always knew it wasn't worth it, that time is too short to be thwarted. One day Natália summed me up with one of those incisive observations of hers: "Grandma's so funny. She always sees the strangeness of the world as a pier to depart from, never as a piece of kitsch to come back to."

These are the advantages of growing up on the brink of war, I think. There were rations, even for people like us, or even especially for people like us, who would never dream of using the sway of our name or our wealth to get a bit more sugar or gasoline. In that way, you and Pedro were exactly like me. Except that you lost everything we had at the roulette table, and I loathed gambling. But I loathed it only because I found all our quarrels over money infinitely tedious. Furthermore, gambling carried the two of you far away from me, and separation is a deep ache to those who perceive the vastness of love compared to the narrowness of life. In any event, when Natália speaks enviously of my slim figure and pale skin, and when I see her come home panting from aerobics, loaded down with firming creams and unsweetened yogurt, apologizing for not being able to try the duck rice I made especially for her, it makes me sad. I'd like for my granddaughter to experience the simple pleasure of walking through that big city she works so hard to expand, in her role as an architect, and afterward, when she gets home, for her to sit on the porch to enjoy a slice of cake with just one egg, with lots of flour and lots of honey to replace the forbidden sugar. I'd like for her to at least believe me when I tell her that if she ever looked up from those magazines she so furiously flips through, she'd discover in men's eyes the matchless beauty of her round body and her cinnamon-colored skin.

But my dear independent Natália, whose life's mission is to liberate women like me from the terrible masculine yoke, will rest in peace only once she achieves the bony slenderness of the haggard adolescents who pass for movie stars in the magazines these days. It makes me sad to see her lose her beauty without even being aware of it, unwittingly becoming a foot soldier in the industry of death that rules the world. They don't make Marilyn Monroes out of Norma Jeanes with hips, bellies, and breasts anymore. And I'm not sure it's fair to put all the blame on men, darling Natália; maybe it's only because men do enjoy the total freedom you feminists are so obsessed with that many of them, despite all claims to the contrary, are still stubbornly capable of loving a woman's cellulite, tears, wrinkles, and wide hips.

Danielle, your real grandmother, was as fat as the full moon when your grandfather fell in love with her. And she was the woman who truly captured his heart, out of the many who fluttered around him.

Danielle was zero percent butterfly. She met Pedro in 1941 as she was rushing with two little girls through Restauradores Square in a sudden summer downpour. He appeared out of nowhere, gallantly offering her an umbrella, and she told him, "If you're a policeman, I wish a bolt of lightning would strike right where you're standing—but I do really appreciate your lending me your umbrella." I remember that sentence just as Danielle recited it to me, and I see Eduardo's body being shattered by lightning, Camila's eyes drying up for good, turning into photographs. Misfortune inscribed in its fullest measure in the very moment of good fortune.

You would mock me, António, I know. Whenever things become linked inside my head with the silent tentacles of a cancer, I feel your mocking laughter sweep through the house. I can't even imagine what would become of me without the company of your laughter at night in this deserted mansion. Danielle loved to laugh about everything and about nothing, defying heaven and polite manners, her head thrown back. The situation wouldn't have been so hard on you if you hadn't refused to meet her. Jealousy is the disease of emotional illiteracy—I think you might even have coined that maxim yourself. Danielle never stole Pedro from you; I spent months with your tears and Camila's, repeating that over and over, and it could have been so easy. Pedro needed the happiness your dark passion lacked, and Danielle needed to leave testimony, and she knew Portugal was the only place where it would be sure to endure. Pedro was very sweet and, most of all, very handsome. He was her last chance.

Danielle was a French Jew who'd fled the Nazis and who was now helping her compatriots—especially women with children—get entry visas to the United States. She intended to emigrate to America herself when her work was finished. But her work was never finished. In 1943, after discovering her parents had been sent to a concentration camp, she became active in the resistance. It was around then that she gave Camila to her father before heading back to France. I remember the moment she arrived on that April 27 as if it were yesterday. Salazar was giving a speech on the national radio station, and I was surreptitiously listening to him, taking notes: "For my part, I am apprehensive, perhaps unjustifiably so, regarding three tendencies in the organization of the world: the push toward optimality—that is, the sway of the unreal in people's aspirations; the impact of war on collectivization habits in daily life; and the primacy of economic matters—that is, the complete subordination of solutions to economic demands, which could turn the world upside down without ever finding the way to peace." I enjoyed listening—I was fascinated by his talent for diplomacy, which was moving us away from war; it seemed to me there was a prophetic lucidity to his analyses of the evolution of the world. Don't yell at me, António; just writing Salazar's name, I sense the air roiling with your anger. Later I hated him as much as you did, especially after what his thugs did to Camila. But blind hatred never does anybody any good.

Danielle's eyes were swollen from crying, and *petite Camille* was wailing on her lap; it seemed she sensed that her mother's lap was going to disappear for good. Danielle placed the girl in my arms and gave me all her most cherished treasures so I could leave them to her daughter: a sheaf of childhood photographs, a pair of pearl earrings, a letter in which she outlined the family's genealogy, and a gold necklace with a Star of David.

At the end of the war, I learned she'd died at Dachau. I heard it from Delfim Veleno, who'd financed the last year of her stay in Portugal. At

first you didn't realize, António, why it is that Pedro and I insisted that
our little Camila, who'd never been baptized, call Veleno her godfather.
Or maybe you suspected later on: you heard many other stories of his
surreptitious generosity. Delfim Veleno was behind the various temporary
jobs that ensured the survival of António Botto, who'd been fired from
the Anthropometric Station of Lisbon's city government and was growing
increasingly ill. Delfim also used to deposit anonymous checks in the bank
account of Josefa's gynecological medicine association, perhaps in memory
of the mother who'd died on him in childbirth. And once he intention-
ally lost a bet to salvage the honor of a diplomat's wife. She was a delicate
girl with large, melancholy eyes, reserved in manner and discreet in dress.
When she was introduced to him, in an effort to be friendly, Delfim swore,
with his usual vehemence, that he'd recently seen her across the room at a
teahouse in Sintra. The diplomat said that was impossible, his wife hadn't
been to Sintra in years. Veleno swore up and down, bet two thousand escudos on the matter, and started giving details. Then he looked at the diplomat's wife and saw that she was pale with panic, near fainting. He pulled
two thousand escudos out of his wallet and gave them to the ambassador:
"I beg your pardon, you are correct. It was most definitely somebody else.
I don't know how I could have mistaken your wife's incomparable beauty.
Please forgive me, my lady. This old man is as blind as a bat."

People are more impressive in their goodness than in their wickedness, so I never grow weary of living. Even now, alone here in these great
empty rooms. In the transparency of solitude, I can observe more clearly
the multiple tones of your soul and the souls of everybody we spent time
with here. And they mingle with the bodies of the living who visit me:
Manuel Almada, Camila, Natália. Maybe that's why everybody leaves
here soothed. I'm a solitary creature, so I've never faced disappointments. I avoid people and observe them from a distance; I never manage to see them from close up, without context. Facing imperfection,
I learned to forgive. I survey the root of people's actions and conclude
that I, too, could have committed them. Even the very worst of them.

5

The last rays of daylight reveal the intimate fervor of things. This was always my favorite time of day. The air seems made of gold; I open the windows to allow the red reflections of the clouds to caress the empty rooms. They're all still just as they were when you were alive, the damask-carpeted staircase lit by tulip-shaped sconces, the library with the book stand in front of your English armchair beside the window, the dining room with the large Italian chandelier glimmering over the immense empire-style table, the walls a jumble of images. The painter Bernardo Marques gave us a watercolor frieze that went all the way around the room. Over the years, the paper the frieze was painted on grew yellow, giving a nostalgic air to those initially too-cheerful figures. Bernardo loved painting landscapes best, but since you weren't a great lover of nature, he thought it more appropriate to reproduce the atmosphere of intellectual salon gatherings in our room.

Even today I laugh remembering the horror etched on my mother's face the first time she visited this house that was once hers and came face-to-face with Max Beckmann's incestuous brother and sister—an oil painting as magnificent as it is barbaric, which you and Pedro had purchased in Berlin back when Beckmann was still a nobody. Standing there at the top of the stairs, she said, "Jenny, have you gone mad? Have you no respect for your father's memory?" Then you appeared, your chest bare beneath the blue silk robe I'd given you as a wedding present, wrapped your arms around my shoulders, and said, "Good morning, Mother-in-Law, dear. I see you're enjoying the changes we've made. Come have a look at the dining room, which I've redubbed the Living Museum of Contrasts." The poor woman was speechless. When she pulled herself back together, she said, "Quite original, I'm sure," and never referred to memory again, whether my father's or anybody else's. When we changed the estate's name from Camellia House to Chess House, she shrugged and said, "You should have just called it Casino—it would have been more accurate."

Neither of us could have dreamed, though, that fifty years later our house would still shock somebody. Camila berated me for placing the leopard skin with gleaming eyes that my father shot in Africa on the hearth. As a little girl, she'd called it "bad kitty" and loved to doze all rolled up in it, staring into the flickering flames, but when she got older and became a hippie, she was embarrassed by it.

As for my sweet Natália, she kills me with her architectonic theorizing: she insists that form should serve function, and she wants to forcibly "minimalize," as she calls it, the house. She thinks I should switch from my bedroom here to the music room downstairs, paint the entire house, sell or put into storage all the furniture and other objects she considers "useless," replace the claw-foot bathtubs with something more practical, remodel the kitchen, replace one of the second-floor bathrooms with another kitchen, and rent out the upper floor. Leave my room, your room, dear António, which I reclaimed only after your death? Over my dead body.

If they'd let me marry Pedro, maybe I'd agree to it. I'd set up two of the rooms for us here on the ground floor; it would seem a little adulterous to have him still sleeping in your bed, without you, after the wedding. Stop laughing, would you? I didn't want him to sleep with me either. In fact, when he asked me to marry him, I told him I'd agree only if we continued to live like brother and sister. "Of course, Jenny," he said. He later confessed, with a melancholy smile, "In any event, my dear, we're too old for such novelties. I don't know if you have ever experienced physical love—nor would I, of course, ask you to confide such a thing in me. But if you have never sampled the delicacies of the flesh, it would be an insult to your radiant sensuality for me to now dare take that privilege. You should know that I have always felt a tender desire for you, and were I not attracted to you, I would not have asked you to be my wife." I stroked his white hair aimlessly the way your fingers used to caress his black hair, and then I kissed him on his eyes, cheeks, and lips with a gentleness that was now only mine and Pedro's. You were there—this time it was you who watched us, deeply moved.

During the long months of the spring of 1988, Pedro and I became very close as we prayed by your bedside, trying to relieve the unspeakable agony of the cancer that was driving you slowly and steadily toward death. The sweetish scent of your illness clung to our bodies, and we interlaced our fingers, which were damp with the tears that flowed from our eyes when you weren't looking. At a certain point we couldn't even tell if you were still looking at us, and, shot through with pain, my heart and Pedro's became a single black mass of gray nerves. You'd be happier knowing that Pedro and I stayed together, António— that's what I tried to make my mother understand. She didn't listen. From the lofty heights of her ninety years, she started treating me like a naïve, useless little girl again, calling me a "feeble lamb" and threatening to kick me out of the house. She was clearly distressed that Camila had officially been made an heir—she would rather have left our estate to distant relatives than to Pedro's family. Over the years she became more and more suspicious of his sincere friendship, António. Only Camila and Natália supported me, but their support was considered immensely suspect: as far as my mother was concerned, Pedro was now just a fortune hunter, and his daughter and granddaughter were stakeholders in our bond. Affronted, Camila demanded to sign away all her inheritance rights, but not even that convinced my mother. And so my mother got her revenge for the Living Museum of Contrasts and the blindness with which I'd hastened into the dashing arms of the man who would squander her fortune and her vanity. And she thereby condemned me to my final solitude, the only one I never chose and that I was never able to endure.

I always used to enjoy being alone in a house full of people. I found the distant murmur of conversations more exciting than the conversations themselves. I often escaped upstairs to breathe in that hot perfume of voices, diluted but intoxicating without any ill effects. I learned to make love alone, on the other side of the wall, watching and listening to the way you made love with Pedro. I even made a peephole in the wall, right beside the dressing table mirror, across from your bed. My fingers would imitate on my body the trail his traced on your body. I'd never realized why the nuns at boarding school always used to come by to make sure we had our hands outside the covers before we went to sleep.

One day the nun made a girl surrender her hidden hands for sniffing, and the girl ended up with thirty lashes of the ruler across her knuckles and a month of punishment. She cried every night, two beds down from mine, but I could never get her to tell me what had been wrong with her hands. Only with your love did I understand. I learned to synchronize my desires and ecstasies with yours; after a while, I even learned to provoke your desire, to pull you toward each other when I wanted to surrender to the divine oblivion of pleasure.

I was always faithful to you, António, however difficult it may be for you now to have that suspicion confirmed. "Why don't you go have a little fun with Manuel Almada, Jennifer?" you used to plead. "I hate seeing you shut up in this big house like a ghost. People should be free. I'd really like for you to have lovers, as other women do."

I replied that I couldn't be like other women just to make you happy, remember? And I pointed out that I also wasn't asking you to be like other men just to make me happy, and that made you really furious. You grabbed me, gave me a kiss on the mouth that was like a slap. "Is this what you want? Are you happy now?" No, that wasn't what I wanted—I wanted you just the way you were. That kind of love was the only thing I could call freedom, and I told you that. But you thought I was being cynical, and I think the idea that you'd turned a confident young woman into a cynic tormented you. Maybe now that all the noises of life are gone from this house, your quiet dead heart can understand that I was very happy here with you.

I never could have clutched at you, António. I think that's why you chose me in the first place: I was light to the touch, slippery as a fish. Only my money carried any weight—a very convenient weight, am I right, my darling? No, I'm not saying you married me for my money. There were plenty of other rich girls ready to lead you to the altar. Of course, without my mother's fortune you wouldn't have even considered me, but without that fortune I myself would be a different person. To isolate a human being's motives and emotions and attempt to analyze them objectively is to perpetrate a profound injustice. In fact, it's because of that supposedly scientific approach, peeling things open so you can look at them up close, that the world is the way it is. Every individual is a harmony of solitude—dismantling the person only mutes that music, makes it inaudible.

I cannot remember the taste of the many kisses I received along these endless corridors, nor the men's names, their smoldering words. My memory is growing as long and sharp as a gramophone needle, ceaselessly repeating the same notes. I remember only that occasion when I felt the damp earth of the lawn yielding beneath my back, the rain lashing my face, and a stranger's head burrowing between my breasts.

It happened during one of the many parties you threw to celebrate the war's end. A casual dinner would be served in the backyard, lit by dozens of lanterns; there were recitations of poems by Lorca, Rimbaud, and Mário de Sá-Carneiro; the straw effigy of a dictator would be set alight; the champagne would flow all night long; and just before sunrise there would be a fireworks display. Every guest was free to invite whomever he wished.

I found myself in the middle of the maze of your botanical chessboard, discussing politics with a Spanish communist I'd never seen before; I had no idea who he was. He'd barely gotten started expounding to an audience of three or four journalists on his marvelous plans for changing the world when I interrupted him, with a defiance that startled even me. "Mark Twain said that teaching others to be good is a noble cause, and much less trouble than being good ourselves," I told him.

His jaw dropped, and he turned his back on his public, offering up an outraged defense as he pursued me through the wavering shadows of the garden. Suddenly a procession of clouds cloaked the stars and the rain began to fall in sheets, soaking my white tulle dress, but I kept arguing, with a heatedness that not even I understood since I generally believed it wasn't worth wasting one's mental energy talking politics. My arguments seemed now to swell with the rain; I fired off pompous asseverations about the concrete injustice that resulted from the abstract notion of equality, until he plugged my mouth with his tongue, put his arms around me, and pulled me down with him onto the ground.

I think the only reason we didn't consummate the act was my own aloof or distracted air. It must have been against his principles to possess a woman who was merely letting herself be taken, without truly participating. The intense physical attraction that had drawn me to him like a magnet when we were debating evaporated once he touched me. I was too used to imagining flesh and was unable to overcome the letdown of the real thing. His caresses became less and less insistent, then bashful, then awkward, until he finally leaped up, excused himself, and fled, trampling the rose beds, heading toward the gate, disappearing into the curtain of water that continued to fall.

But my most vivid memory of that night is still the memory of your eyes lingering on me with unexpected fascination. I was coming up the path from the lake, muddy and dazed, and you turned your head and stared at me like an unfinished statue. You forgot about the person standing before you and moved toward me, wavering. You stopped a few feet away and poured the slow flame of your gaze onto my body. I saw our whole life, past and future, parading in a spiral around us, as if the universe were ending right there. Then you said, "Such beauty drives a man to wish for death, Jennifer."

On hot spring nights, as an unexpected rain tumbles down onto the earth, I run out into the garden in search of you. I know they say I'm going mad. That may be true, but they discovered it too late.

A few days ago, Natália came to ask me to lend her our theater costumes for a Carnival party she's hosting. I told her she would be inheriting all of the trunks—it's written in my will. Even so, I can't bear to let go of them while I'm still alive. "But it's only for two weeks, Grandma," she said. Natália lives her life at top speed, but she doesn't see that two weeks is a huge amount of time. In those two weeks, your Knight of the Round Table costume would take on the form and odor of another body and would no longer belong to me.

Pedro was King Arthur, and Hamlet, and Romeo, and King Pedro the Cruel. We always gave Veleno the role of the shield bearer or conspirator, and he enjoyed resounding success as Cardinal Cerejeira in the play *The Wise Man and His Saint*, written by you and Pedro. Later, though, he swore up and down that he'd never agreed with those "subversive ravings" and insisted it had been Manuel Almada who'd played the cardinal. I think he never forgave Manuel the magnanimities of wealth.

"You don't have any use for those clothes, Grandma," Natália said, and left in a huff. How can I explain that I need only that which is useless? She'd never understand. She married a young man who is supremely useful. They split the mortgage on their shared house and two individual cars; he cooks and she loads the dishwasher; they support each other through the hard times; they enjoy the same movies, books, and records; and most of all, she claims, they "respect each other's space."

If it hadn't been Natália, and if it weren't blasphemous, I would have said amen when she came to me, euphoric, to enumerate this list of positive qualities and invite me to the wedding. But instead I just asked whether she was in love with him. She laughed at me. She stroked my cheek but laughed at me, and explained that women today aren't so foolish as to get married for love. She said statistics have shown that love marriages end after a few years. A psychologist friend of hers confirmed this finding and claimed that the basis for a successful relationship lies in "shared interests and aspirations." The last rays of summer sunlight were coming in through the window, lengthening the shadows and briefly setting the row of photographs on the side table aflame. "Of course, physical compatibility is important too," Natália continued, "but nowadays nobody gets married blindly, without experience. In the year and a half we've been living together, it's been clear that we get along. Ultimately, a wedding is a formality. It's just a party. Aren't you happy for me?" A gust of wind rattled the doors, ruffled the trees, and frightened the birds outside, which twittered madly. "I am; I'm really happy for you, Natália. And what about Álvaro?"

Natália had donned the black habit of love at thirteen years old, and at eighteen she'd fulfilled most of that vow with Álvaro, a short lad with stooped shoulders who worked in an art gallery, wore hobnail boots, and had a ponytail. When she told me that this modern Adonis drove her mother wild, I chided her. But Natália replied just as I would have in the same situation: "Love isn't fair, Jenny. Not for me either." In any case, she was discreet enough to keep the romance far from Camila's view. I ended up accepting the role of Natália's confidant without guilt, believing that Álvaro's timid utilitarianism—he'd once described painting as "the production of chromatic efficiencies" or something along those lines—would have had a devastating effect on Camila's rigid spirit. Natália, though, thrived on their disagreements. Annoyed, she'd retort, "All art is emotion. Every idea that occurs to us is carried in our blood."

Now, five years later, she was wrinkling her forehead with her mother's curt furrow. "What did I see in Álvaro?" "I don't know. Have you forgotten already?" It must have been vengeance—when I contemplate it, I think that's what it was—though there was no remedying the situation by that point. Annoyed at the condescending way she'd stroked my cheek, I was tempted to remind her of the nights I'd spent wiping away her tears and listening to her go on about Álvaro. I wanted to remind her of the times she'd confessed, "I want old-fashioned emotions, Jenny, with a capital *E*, with rules and concrete evidence!" I missed those nights when she'd talk to me about the love of men in a language that I could understand, without hedging or statistics.

Natália got up and started pacing irritably back and forth, saying the relationship had been over for a while now and she and Álvaro were just good friends because she'd decided she didn't have time to waste on *losers*—she used the English word. I thought about my mother and Delfim Veleno, who also loved foreign words and hadn't had time to waste on losers either. I looked over at Natália, her thick hair gleaming and her eyes glinting with determination, and felt sad. I told her I'd like to buy her wedding dress for her. "It's not worth it," she said. "It's crazy to buy a dress you can only wear once. I bought a light-blue suit, really beautiful, and I'll be able to use it again afterward." I told her white might have been a better choice, and she got offended. "Why? Because I'm dark-skinned?" "Yes, Natália, because white sets off the magnificent coffee color of your skin," I said. "Plus, to me, brides always wear white." She hugged me repentantly. Then she said it had seemed hypocritical to dress up as a virgin.

I thought of Josefa Nascimento at fifty-two years old, a widow and now a bride for the second time—this time to a lawyer who ended up dying soon after of a heart attack—more beautiful than she'd ever been, garbed in white lace and a veil and holding a cigar, in 1954. Camila was the ring bearer, with Carlinhos de Sousa as her escort. Carlinhos was a charming boy—when he was a teenager we'd started calling him Carlos Bonito, "pretty-boy Carlos"—who followed her everywhere and was frequently punished by his mother for surreptitiously emptying the contents of her box of ginger candy to give them to Camila. Josefa spent her whole life trying to convince women that purity is a state of mind, but it seems that the literal will always win out. So I told Natália I wanted to provide the wedding rings. She refused, declaring them a symbol of captivity.

I ended up giving her the gold watch you gave me as a wedding present, António. She was touched, and I think she liked it. I did try to persuade her to have the reception here at the house, but she wanted to hold it "somewhere modern."

Regrettably, António, what Natália calls "somewhere modern" is an enormous white tent draped with heavy yellow ribbons. The chairs and tables were also made of white cloth with yellow ribbons. Even the roses—just imagine—were white and yellow. Camila was annoyed about the absurd quantities of ribbons and yellow too, but she told me that's what people do these days. It's only at times like these that I realize I've grown old. I spend my days nostalgically recalling the many weddings we held here at the house during the sixties and seventies.

To keep you away from the casinos, where your hands shook and our love was tainted, I turned our music room into a bar, organizing an ongoing salon that would bind you to the house, and to me. It was also, I confess, a way of making a little money, since our dinner parties and your gambling were driving us into bankruptcy. At the time, money was a trifling thing that, if it were ever lacking, would emerge naturally from the pocket of some friend, or even a mere acquaintance. Above all, people valued the pleasure of social interaction and worried about to-day's little luxuries rather than the major profits of invisible tomorrows.

Josefa gave us our first stock of drinks, and Manuel Almada the counter and benches, and the only reason Delfim Veleno didn't install a television in the bar was because you refused: "Fascist television, no way!" Veleno shot back smugly, "You're just jealous because my daughter is a TV star!" The so-called star was, at the time, just a presenter—it was only after the revolution that she landed her interview program, *Glory with Glória*—and you couldn't help laughing. But the bar managed to draw you back home, and your laughter glowed in the windows and mirrors late into the night, rivers of light flowing even today over the stillness of my heart.

Once, during our wedding-venue period, a girl showed up wearing orange stilettos, jeans, and a cotton T-shirt with the English word *Class* embroidered in sequins across the chest, and carrying a rolled-up magazine tucked under her arm. She opened the magazine to a dog-eared spread and told me she wanted a wedding just like that one. It was the wedding of Princess Anne of England and Captain Mark Phillips. I told her it would be tough but we could do something similar, and she was satisfied with that. You and Pedro used to flee the house whenever we organized those new-money weddings right out of the pages of a magazine. You'd adopt a distant, superior air, which is just shame in disguise.

On the morning of her exceedingly logical wedding, Natália was sweating so much that we couldn't get her dressed. I suggested she postpone everything until she was feeling better. Natália and Camila were horrified—after spending all that money and inviting dozens of guests, the bride couldn't back out, not even for an emergency. It was just nerves, perfectly normal. On the morning of our wedding, António, I awoke radiantly serene, rehearsing the "I do" that would bring my dream to fruition.

Midway through the afternoon, Álvaro, whom I'd still never met in person, pulled off one of the bows from the chairs and started dancing around with it, shouting that marriage was the chicest form of hanging. They kicked him out into the street, and Natália instantly lost her will to laugh and dance.

Now she's started smoking again. I scold her out of a sense of obligation, but without conviction. The smell of smoke clings to the house's walls longer than her ever-changing perfume. I leave the butts in the ashtrays awhile to preserve her presence. I did the same thing with your cigarettes, António—when you and Pedro went away, I used to forbid Rosário to clean the ashtrays.

6

In the summertime we'd rent a house at the seaside. In Espinho or Figueira da Foz, because of the casino. The war meant we couldn't set our sights on other countries; instead, we tried to dilute our longing for travel in the motion of the waves. You and Pedro would come home at sunrise, propping each other up, telling me you'd gambled away another of my sets of English china, and you'd go to bed as I headed out to the beach.

People weren't tanning back then, but we also hadn't invented the ozone hole or skin cancer yet. I'd settle down to read a novel till the sun was searing my blood, and then plunge into the icy waves. I'd swim in the current, cutting through the foam, until the marrow of my bones had turned to ice. My low-cut bathing suit upended all the tame seaside conventions. I wanted to merge with the sun and the water—if it wouldn't have caused an uproar, I'd have lounged on the sand naked. It is only with regard to conventions such as these that I envy Camila's generation. And I got my revenge: she was the first girl to run around naked on these beaches, which were full of children all wrapped up like old presents. There was a man who, at prearranged times, would grab the shrieking packages and casually dunk them in the sea, indifferent to the children's yelps of terror, while the mothers kept crocheting and placidly chatting, gathered in the blue-and-white-striped tents. That technique, it was thought, would bolster the children's health and courage. Most of the members of that generation who experienced forced sea-bathing as children refused to learn to swim.

The sea always used to soothe Camila—she was a nervous child whose emotions alternated between ecstasy and despair. She asked endless questions: "Mother Jenny, if the Earth is round and all full of water, how come it doesn't spill?" She could go from laughter to tears in an instant. I spent years worrying that this innate excess would rip her life to pieces. And so it did, but above all it dried her up inside so thoroughly that even now I find it hard to believe. I miss her laughter, which used to come in steady swells, like the sea; I miss the joy that flooded her over the most trivial matter—a spoon, a pot lid, a trip to the café, a ride on her father's back, a fistful of sand.

All it took to make her weep disconsolately was raising your voice in public. Countless arguments between you and Pedro were cut off that way, by the force of her tears. She could be sitting quietly on the other side of the room, absorbed in the universe of her toys, and then, as your voices started growing louder, she would make the walls shake with fury and anguish.

When she came back home after spending a month in prison when she was eighteen, rage was still smoldering in the depths of her gray eyes. A dark rage, reptilian in its stillness, no longer the least bit naïve. Veleno had stammered that he couldn't do anything, that Camila had been caught red-handed distributing subversive pamphlets; these were unsettled times, he said, and we had to keep in mind that he had a daughter to take care of too. Delfim Veleno had ended up blowing with the political winds and marrying the doe-eyed daughter of a general with ties to the regime. From that marriage came a daughter they named Glória, who was hell-bent on living up to her name. After Camila's stint in prison, I was never able to speak to Veleno again. I would remember his round head self-assuredly wagging: "Please understand, I can't risk my career over your daughter's wild whims. Ask for anything but that. Plus, our police force is lenient—nothing bad is going to happen to her. Maybe the scare will even do her good—young people need discipline." It was Manuel Almada—who'd managed to keep one foot in the regime so he could help his friends, and both hands in the resistance, writing, frittering away a fortune on underground publications and signing checks for the cause of freedom—who ended up getting them to release Camila.

The communist leader Álvaro Cunhal escaped from prison at the beginning of that year, 1960, and the police made up for that loss with a thorough sweep for opposition figures. The flooding in the Ribatejo region in March complicated things, producing a raft of dead bodies to be gotten rid of in an effort to preserve Portugal's image of sun-drenched tranquility. In addition, progress was on the move: Lisbon's subway system opened, as did the Portuguese-French Cultural Institute at the Gulbenkian Foundation in Paris. And you had to be particularly cautious with intellectuals, who might stymie a nation's grand plans just for the pleasure of coming up with extravagant slogans. As for Camila, she was fascinated with Khrushchev's new style.

I never learned exactly what they did to her during that month in prison. All she told me was that Carlos Bonito would interrogate her day and night, endlessly, until she passed out, in the cells of the secret police on Rua António Maria Cardoso. As children the two of them had spent entire afternoons together, playing blindman's buff in the garden. From a distance, he looked like the Nordic incarnation of the myth of beauty: blond, tall, broad shoulders, narrow hips, the soft-focus face of an angel. But whenever he kissed my hand, I'd always felt a sort of uneasy chill. His flawless hand, tipped with delicate fingernails tinged a flawless pink, was limp and sticky to the touch. His lips, drawn with a T square and painted in watercolors, were as cold as a marble gravestone, and his eyes had stolen the blue from the sky, emptying it of light. He was the real-life harbinger of the machine-man, programmed to eradicate any obstacle to the victory of pure form. From a very young age he'd boasted of casting off books, movies, knowledge, and emotions. At first Camila found him amusing; later she felt sorry for him. She fell into the trap of empathy, as so many intelligent people do out of an audacious generosity: she thought that steely layer of staunch beauty masked a woeful sense of inferiority. But the only thing masked by Carlos's beauty was that beauty's will to triumph.

I think Camila could have made it through without falling apart if, over the course of those torturous days, Carlos had acted out of vengeful resentment. With her head resting in my lap, staring up at the ceiling, in a pale voice that no longer sounded like hers, Camila told me, "The worst part, Jenny, was the calm way he'd light his cigarettes, smiling and saying he didn't have anything against me, it was nothing personal, he was just doing his job." She requested that I not ask any more questions. From then on, it was as if she were sleepwalking. We'd try to cheer her up, drag her out to shows or on walks, but she'd only repeat these four words: "It doesn't make sense."

Carlos Bonito was proof that human evil existed as an autonomous, uncontainable monster rather than being, as Camila had previously believed, a consequence of the poverty resulting from capitalist competition. She lost her faith, abandoned her militant activism. And the party abandoned her too; an asset who had been captured by the secret police was burned, a threat to the continuing fight. You and Pedro sighed with relief: "Better for her to be depressed than in prison." For my part, I honestly preferred her at risk and euphoric rather than safe and unhappy. "She's too young to deny her true nature," you'd say. "She's a passionate person. She's like me, see, Pedro?" You'd laugh. "Through some intricate stratagem, genetics has remedied the shortcomings of standard reproduction methods—your daughter takes after me."

Yes, Pedro's daughter took after us, António, me and you, the fervent ones. And when she fell for Eduardo she discovered in fervency the hint of a new universal harmony, more contagious and easier to achieve than unreliable material equality.

"He's massive," Camila said the first time she saw him. She was reluctantly accompanying me to *The Place Where Time Ended*, a play written and directed by an extraordinarily tall twenty-year-old who seemed embarrassed by the stir he'd created. At the end of the performance, Camila stood up suddenly to take photographs, and the camera corrected that initial impression: he wasn't intimidated by being photographed. Eduardo was the sort of person who doesn't need to mug for the camera or say thank you, which gave the portrait a strangely authentic air. He was a serious young man. That seriousness came across in his voice, deep and gloomy like a piece of old sheet music. It took a while to decipher his words because it was almost impossible to separate them from the voice that uttered them. And also because he preferred difficult words. Or maybe he just hadn't found the other ones yet, the words of revelation.

I think the two of them fell for each other that very night. We went back to the dressing room to congratulate one of Manuel Almada's nieces who'd been part of the cast, and Eduardo invited us to have dinner with him. It seemed like the start of a classic romance, with only the characters and settings altered. Nobody had chaperones anymore, much less thought someone like Camila might need one. "You two go on," I told her. "You're young." But Camila pried open my hand with her sweaty fingers and murmured, using the informal *tu*, "Don't think you're getting out of this, Jenny. You made me come, so now I'm making you." She took that tone with me only when she was feeling either very anxious or very cheeky.

Caught off guard by the turmoil in her heart, she was trying to pretend nothing was going to happen. Eduardo launched into a monologue and suddenly lost his train of thought midsentence. He wasn't afraid of getting lost; he knew it was the price of disquiet. He wasn't even afraid of being misunderstood. But he'd learned as a boy to be well mannered and affable, so he took pains to apologize for his "excessively abstract" thoughts. Certainly Eduardo never had descriptive conversations. He used to say he had no patience for people who interacted only at that level. He could have taken Rimbaud as his model: "I have come to see as sacred the disorder of my spirit."

The Place Where Time Ended was the first show in which he'd done it all: conception, sets, direction, acting. "This play is about consciousness. The setting is the nation, shattered by immobility. And a fragmented self in search of its own memory." Camila listened, her gray eyes shining like silver, entranced. "I'm very nihilistic. There are a lot of people waiting. The world is in a desperate situation, and the theater is a way of exorcising those forces." Pedro said she was seeking in art the salvation that politics had not provided. But it wasn't that. Camila was no longer looking for salvation. She was in love, shielded from the world's disappointments. And then a year later, as he was coming out of the sea, Eduardo was struck by lightning and killed. Saying that Portugal was a magnet for death, Camila flew to Mozambique to work as a correspondent for a newspaper as soon as the war started. She passionately chased after death, and she found it again in Xavier, the soldier from the Mozambique Liberation Front who deposited Natália's life in her belly.

7

Everyone who dies burrows into the walls of the house and perches in the treetops in the garden. At first I thought they'd keep me company. In the spring of 1988, when you died, António, and Pedro left, your nervous footsteps made the night explode with fallen leaves. I would sit out on the porch in silence to feel you close to me. After you came into the house, your laughter would shred the suffocating cloak of unwanted solitude. Eleven months later, Pedro died—he couldn't bear being in that nursing home.

Still, I went to see him once. He asked me not to come back. He had tremors in his hands, and he was embarrassed by the smell of urine and by the old people around him who served to confirm his decline. He played solitaire and even played himself in chess. I was almost happy to hear of his death, especially because I started to hear his voice, beneath yours, asking you to protect me. Rosário died a few months ago; I'd assumed she was immortal because she'd been there at my birth. When it was clear the time was approaching, she said goodbye and went home to her family in the village. Now she sings her old fados all night long, down in the kitchen. But your voices, which were such a comfort to me, only amplified the lack of life in this house. They are solemn and vague; they speak of eternity, disregarding the tiny moments that compose a life.

During the summer we used to have lunch out on the porch. You and Pedro, only recently risen and still in your dressing gowns, would scan the newspapers, drinking milky coffee and eating scrambled eggs. Sometimes you commented on the aroma of the soup or stew that Camila and I were eating. At night there was always somebody over for dinner—Josefa or Manuel or a pal from the casino. You always found fault with the food—the eggs weren't fresh, or the veal was too well done, or maybe it was the wine, which was never the right temperature. Pedro never had a problem with anything, and as soon as he sat down, he'd start looking for the two hottest eggs or the best piece of meat to put on your plate. I miss these little particulars, the quarrels over a spotty wineglass or a bit of gossiping about our friends. And it is in these little particulars that memory is concentrated, casting such an intense light on those distant days that I sometimes fear they're no longer memories but instead pure figments of my solitude. I don't know what I had for lunch today, but I remember in minute detail every experience and every dream from that time when I was happy.

Delfim Veleno's grand projects, for example. When the war ended, he got it into his head to start a bilingual newspaper, in Portuguese and English, called *A Opinião/The Opinion*, which aimed to publish the world's most prominent reporters. He was eager to make contact with embassies, printers, and wealthy tycoons. He managed to persuade a wine producer in Porto to put out a slightly different publication, *The Varietals' Opinion*, in which international politics alternated elegantly with images of Portuguese wine production, and he came to us euphoric, urging us to collaborate in this outstanding "project of Lusitanian expansion."

Three weeks later, he showed up at the house at noon—you and Pedro were still yawning, bleary-eyed—and announced, "*Bambini*, I've got a wonderful idea, magnificent, sublime. I know, I know, you'd expect nothing less. I'm thinking of creating the Contemporary Museum of Anonymous Greats, full of photographs, paintings, and documents donated by anonymous heroes, illustrating everyday events from around the world or the nation during this century. I've already done a sketch of the building and everything. Because of course it would be best to build something from scratch that will be worthy of the project. I'm going to talk to the minister. Have a look." We had a look. It was a sort of re-creation of the Temple of Diana in Évora, with a profusion of brawny gods and lyre-playing muses atop each column. "If this won't work, that's all right. We can use a place that's already built and change the facade. I've got it all figured out." Pedro asked, "What about the newspaper?" Veleno shrugged, irritated: "It's a rip-off, my friend, a total rip-off. Would you believe the winemaker wanted all the odd-numbered pages to be ads for his beverages? All of them. Every single one—can you imagine such a thing? I told him that no editorial by Delfim Velleno was ever going to be hidden away on an even-numbered page, and I left it to him. Plus, it was going to be a pretty pitiful operation—total shoestring. The man wanted to flay me alive. But not Delfim Velleno, never, and that's what I told him. Anyway, water under the bridge. Running a newspaper's a pain. There are plenty of them already—maybe too many."

A few years later he was all set to make a "fresh, original, *gorgeous*" film that would take place entirely in Portugal dos Pequenitos, that children's theme park in Coimbra, with children playing the lives of adults; our daughters were to be the stars. And through all these activities, the epic of his never-ending novel continued. That project's aim was to "sketch the definitive portrait of our generation and eclipse all previously written words." He had, over the years, come up with a solid dozen titles and a few possible plots, depending on his outrage of the moment. All for naught. As you once said, António, "The tribulations of existence will not permit that literary masterpiece to emerge from the brilliant prison of the mind that produced it."

In 1954, as the turmoil over Portugal's possessions in Goa increased, Veleno was offered a promotion in exchange for denouncing subversives. The opposition, which now supported keeping the territory, carped about the way the government was handling the conflict, and the Communist Party passed out a flyer that heaped criticism on Salazar and called for Goan self-determination. Salazar went on and on about how Goa was "a light of the West in eastern domains" and, during one of our long evenings together, Delfim was the first to laugh at the phrase: "That's a typo, my friends, a major typo. Instead of 'domains,' he meant 'dimness.' As good old Boots Salazar sees it, the East begins at the Spanish border, and it's a very dark place."

On those nights when we held our salon, all kinds of people talked freely about all manner of subjects. At one point a somewhat intoxicated infantry major started passing out a pamphlet for the Communist Party, claiming a coup d'état was in the offing that would put an end to the fascist puppet show. Two days later, the man was arrested for conspiracy, and Delfim, who was the only regime official in the group, was expelled from our salons by unanimous decision. You were the only one to defend him, António. Veleno gave the situation a dramatic cast—"It was him or me," he said, "they suspected me, said I was consorting with subversives, demanded evidence"—and six months later he was awarded a medal and a promotion. Not even Pedro could understand why you forgave Veleno, why you continued to see him behind everyone's back; for several months Pedro almost stopped speaking to you. We spent many a sleepless night, Pedro inexorably calm in the face of your pleading and kisses, giving in to your violent fits of desire with the indifference with which a tree or a bit of land submits to a storm, and me, glued to the wall in the room next door, focusing all my strength on Pedro, praying for the ball of ice that had formed around his heart to melt, for his body to requite, in my name, your passion.

I was never able to forgive Delfim, but I came to accept him again. I managed to look at him through the bright light of your friendship. In using cowardice to pursue his ambitions, Delfim had become dangerous. But he would never betray a friend, and who among us, in those days of terror, would refuse to turn in a stranger if we thought our own life depended on it? Those were your arguments, shot through with the golden threads of an old affection and laden with fundamental compassion. At the height of the 1974 revolution, many people turned in lifelong friends for much less. Today, in this cartoon of a democratic paradise, nobody turns in anybody; people, having become more sophisticated, have learned to sell themselves out instead. They simply abandon anyone without the means to pay to be forgotten. "I can't stand with you on this. I have too much to lose, and nothing to gain. But at least I admit it," said Glória Veleno when Camila needed her testimony. Glória always admits to everything—*admit* is actually one of her favorite verbs, and everybody praises her candor. Her father, at least, was ashamed to admit to his selfishness and spent a lot of time making up lies to avoid hurting anyone deliberately; he lived during a time in which the "too much" that could be lost was one's freedom and even, sometimes, one's life. There was something generous and buttressing in the megalomania of Delfim Veleno's endeavors. He needed to make everything around him vibrate in order to be happy. He spent weeks on diplomatic missions of reconciliation, attempting to heal the wounds that your intense moodiness opened within our group of friends.

In the end, after Camila's stay in prison, we cut Veleno out of our lives for good, and the house gradually emptied out once there was nobody willing to act as a peacemaker when you were sulking. Manuel Almada's gentleness was intense but static; he would sit down somewhere to observe the disputes, listening carefully to the accusations lobbed from each trench without ever taking a side. And gradually I noticed that he was actually pleased that people were abandoning the house—it made us all the more dependent on his unshakable friendship.

As these events were imperceptibly unfolding over the years, I reassessed my feelings about Delfim Veleno, and I think at this point I have forgiven him for his terrible inaction in the face of what they did to Camila. In fact, I think Delfim had no idea what really happened in those interrogation rooms. But you were able to be merciful earlier than I, António. You remained blind, resolutely dazzled by the bright light of a shared memory, and you stayed by Delfim's side despite everyone else's opinions. You said opinions were like spare parts and sometimes stood in for principles when the latter ran out. Yet the joy of Camila's presence had reconciled you with Danielle's role, and a couple dozen times a day you pointed out to Pedro that without Delfim's help, Danielle might not have been able to carry her daughter to full term. Gratitude served as an anchor, reminding us that the sea had a bottom just as suffering would have an end.

Camila and Natália deploy this anchor, dropping it into nostalgia for their projects: photographs, houses. Things that last. When I was young, changes were slow and piecemeal. A swarm of the living crowded around the dead to drink in that shared grief. Everything was close: opulence, poverty, passion, despair, infamy, decency, all parading before us in a slow, circular procession, and we tarried there, dissecting all of their manifestations. It was only much later that television leveled out everything in a fluid language for which violence was the only Esperanto.

We were meek because we remembered; violence consumed us like a transgression. I pulled its garments aside to reveal its privates and indulged in it to escape the stultifying rituals of women's mummified lives. Living meant endlessly remembering, ad nauseam, repaying visits, celebrating births and deaths, writing dozens of postcards on a single weekend away, nurturing Christmas dreams, painting eggs at Easter, honoring the wounded, the maimed, and all the other inheritors of human madness. As the new century approached, the vertigo of forgetting was chewed up by the vertigo of remembering. But it's a futurist Carnival, with the powerful men of today dressed up as intergalactic voyagers, philosophizing about the discoveries the future would bring, or with choristers playing mermaids and comedians in the role of Camões.

I never used to like commemorations—they anesthetize the work of the mind. But now I find them nearly irresistible. Melancholy hijacks my youth and raises it aloft, like a tattered flag, atop the skyscrapers that cast shadows and scorn over your botanical chessboard, António. The trees you had trimmed in the shape of statues now have shaggy beards, unkempt hair, crooked arms that tangle together as if trying to prop each other up. Now there is only one gardener, too old for tree trimming. He looks after the pansies, roses, and hydrangeas, while the rest of the garden turns to jungle. The grass has grown taller than the flowers, the boxwoods are withering, oranges rot on the ground. And this jungle speaks. When the wind whistles through the mass of leaves the chess garden has become, the noises and voices of old emerge once more. The clinking of utensils and glasses, the bustling of the girls in the kitchen, presided over by Rosário's high-pitched voice, an unidentified exclamation of horror, Camila's lullabies.

You whisper to me, tell me I'm crazy. Maybe you're right. But I'm no crazier than I was that night when, furious at your indifference, I dreamed of hiring two male servants and entering the dining room reclining on a cushion of lilies upon a silver platter, naked, with an apple in my mouth.

8

I always hated it when you gambled. Sweat would start beading your brow with your very first bet. You'd pull out your handkerchief and vigorously rub your face.

The gesture was not just crude but also pointless: the sweat grew like a tumor, gleaming, uncontrollable; it trickled down the nape of your neck, slicked your hands. Water leaked from your eyes, which became glassy; you were a celluloid puppet melting with the heat. In the gambling dens, Pedro was the man of your dreams, firmly straightening the cards with masterful fingers, grinning at the croupier, gently warding off the trophy hunters. Some were soul-sad men who, in their sadness, aspired to a perfected extreme of feminine beauty. They walked gingerly, as if they, too, were sworn to the brutal pact of femininity embraced by Andersen's little mermaid and with every step felt a thousand blades stabbing through their luster-paper facade and into their flesh. I don't know how they managed to achieve the gorgeous figure of the ideal woman in a time when plastic surgery was still something out of science fiction.

Nowadays they get silicone breast implants, paint themselves up like Carnival masks, and wander through the streets at dawn, living dead doomed to purgatory. In those ancient days they seemed to be born of the light from the jewels and gold that scattered across the green felt. They deceived men flawlessly, and in the end those men threw themselves at their feet, renouncing a lifetime of committed virility for their love. "Don't embarrass me in public," the women would tell their suitors, shoving their heads with the toe of a glossy sandal. "I don't want to be seen with a fag."

I remember one of them in particular, Eleonor, who, after calmly shooing away a tearful bullfighter, started venting to me. Coiling the ringlets that framed her clear blue eyes around her right thumb, she described her persistent bad luck with men: they'd be stable and sturdy at first, able to fight off three armies with one arm while protecting her with the other, but after a couple of days they'd turn into fussy infants and want her to swaddle them. "That's the way it always goes—I make them go soft. It must be my way of making up for not being able to have children. I'm sterile—you can't imagine how agonizing that is. Yet another reason to want a real man who makes me feel like any other woman—one who asks me to be his wife, not his mother, don't you think?" Her sad story began with a violent father and a hasty, mistake-ridden marriage. Afterward, loneliness had drawn her to gambling, and gambling to straying men. By the end of the night, she was giving me recipes for concoctions to lighten my complexion and making up my eyes "in a more spiritual way."

I hated seeing you gamble—I'd dog you through those opulent rooms to see you disfigured, trying to love you with moderation. Eventually I came to despise you; I couldn't bear myself because my feelings for you were simply my feelings. Love doesn't have doors that we can open and shut, or secret passageways to a cellar where we can take a break from it. Love takes us over completely, wraps us up like a shroud of tedium, silky, infinite. Nobody talks about that sublime tedium, the opposite of action and efficacy, immobile enemy of progress in the world. It is only on the gleaming and dismal throne of dreams that love stimulates. If prolonged, life becomes too short and love acquires the rhythm of rain softly, softly beating down. We are used to treating love affairs like appliances: when they break down, we go to the store to buy a new one identical to the other one. Fix it? It's not worth it: repairs are expensive, plus it's hard to know where to get replacement parts.

We substituted repetition for eternity, and the world began to become as monotonous as practicing scales on the piano. We feared the greatest giddiness of all: the idea that things might last. But every endeavor eventually ends with a cemetery like Romeo and Juliet's, though the atmosphere may differ—and atmosphere is, after all, the most important thing. People are dying older and more exhausted, and their rigid corpses sink ludicrously beneath the soil of their ephemeral triumphs.

I became aware that I was going to die the day that, for the first time, I looked in the mirror and recognized myself. I knew about my death even before I knew how to express myself properly. Children these days already know how to do calculations and operate computers before they know who they are and where they came from. They're taught to walk earlier and earlier; they don't even go through the crawling stage anymore. When I was a little girl, there were always a lot of people slowly dying, passing down to their descendants the tranquil witnessing of their death. The dead were young and slow; they loomed over the living like guardian angels, muting their triumphs and envies, making their lives' most pressing aspects seem ridiculous. The men died earlier than the women, and with less of the glory of being remembered, which is the only true glory. The women stuck more in our memory because they lived on the fringes of men's struggle for the things of the earth. Men spent their time accumulating wealth and land that persisted after them, mocking, in their eternal quietude, the tenuous existence of those who had amassed them. When a woman died, she took her talent for jam making and her singular way of loving with her. She left behind nothing that diminished her.

You used to say, "Reason is the domain of the female sex; emotion, that of the male." You were trying to needle me, and you succeeded. You had a knack for raising my hackles in a flash: "So be it. Good sense may not shine bright or roar loudly, but the treasures of the spirit have the supreme advantage of being impossible to steal."

I found a childish consolation in those aphoristic duels with you, which brought us closer and warmed us like a vice surreptitiously shared in the midst of a crowd. In his jealousy, Pedro became more affectionate; our exchanges both unnerved and fascinated him. At a certain point, Josefa Nascimento started going around with a little notebook so she could jot down our repartee, and sometimes she'd try to get us going: "Nobody has any scathing opinions today to add some pizzazz to Mr. Birth's criminal element?" You always fell for it: "I reject the miserable custom of having opinions; I prefer to live on thoughts and emotions."

I loved you fiercely on those nights of long, impassioned, vital conversations about the meaning of history and the roots of identity. "Portugal's glory came out of our nation's insistence on doubling the world until it matched its dreams," you'd say. "Or transforming its nightmares into a romantic, pocket-size memory," I'd add. Manuel Almada would smooth things over: "Portugal resisted decline again and again, cocooning itself away, passionately committed to patience, which can always scoff at larger passions." And I remember one occasion when Bernardo Marques, who sometimes turned up at the house with Manuel Almada, said that the Portuguese soul was made of tile, painted and chipped.

Back then, there were terrible rumors about Josefa going around; people were saying that the only reason she wasn't in prison for being a communist was that she was having an affair with a government minister. She was unfazed by notoriety, but her good humor turned to pure sarcasm. "Chipped tiles—no kidding! The Portuguese know better than to get caught up in insoluble conflicts. They gossip to avoid brawling, conspire instead of murdering, deny themselves in order to assert themselves. In Portugal, a person is better compensated for being the victim of malicious rumors than for being the victim of a crime.

The evidence of that goes all the way back to King Sebastian. If the North Africans had packed him off back to where he came from, he never would have acquired such luster. People always suspect that a crime victim has, at the very least, put up an inadequate self-defense—which is itself a way of abetting the criminal."

Manuel Almada argued that Portuguese small-mindedness was the result of the country's position off the main highways of history: "It's both an advantage and a disadvantage. An advantage because history leaves a trail of blood behind it wherever it goes. And a disadvantage because history also leaves a trail of creativity." "Look," Josefa replied, "history bears the entire world on its broad shoulders, and when people don't have anywhere else to place the blame, they place it there—there's plenty of room." I remember Josefa once shouting angrily at Manuel Almada for having attempted to placate her rage at "frustrated men who can't stand seeing a woman making a mark." On that occasion you surprised even me: "Yes indeed, Josefa," you said gravely. "It makes me proud to hear you talk like that. To me, each obedient submissive is a dictator who's just waiting for the winds of history to position him to trade his silent hatred for bloodbaths."

Despising you, António, meant despising myself, and the red-hot lava of that contempt might have blackened my love but did not burn it, because love is naturally fireproof. Once, Natália asked me, "What was your relationship with Grandpa António like, Grandma?" I laughed and said, "Thank God, sweetheart, António and I never had what you'd call a relationship. In fact, when we got married, the word didn't even exist." Natália stared at me, taken aback. She is baffled by anything that doesn't come out of well-ordered individualism, feels sorry for it—and just as well. As long as she remains distracted by her attempts to hurt me, she will not examine her own heart, from which she has voluntarily distanced herself. Maybe she's better off living that way; the Álvaro who showed her what love is didn't actually seem able to bear up under the everlasting weight of that gift. The rapid pace that governs the world does not allow anything to elude its command: people mate as if they were going in together on buying high-quality shoes at wholesale in order to make money faster than they could on their own. You always were able to honor our commitment, to accept the absolute inflexibility of my soul in yours. Even described thus, that must seem so paltry in modern terms, because there's nothing modern about it—and yet it fills my life with light, and will persist in the shadows of the heavens after the banality of my death.

9

A new restaurant has opened across the street from our house. The owner's husband sits out on the sidewalk every day. He tidies his car, rummages in the trunk and pulls out a little bench, a box of brushes, tubes of paint, an easel, and starts painting the people eating lunch by the front window. He's tall, slender, quite young—twenty-five, twenty-seven at most. I heard them one morning with her yelling, "Scram! Go away and don't come back!" before hurling the pigments at the nearly finished painting. He set the canvas aside and started a new one.

Later, by chance, I saw the story on television, on a midday news program. The restaurant owner was accusing the young painter, whom the caption identified with the ignominious title of *ex-husband*, of sexual harassment. He responded that it was impossible for him to become her ex-husband because he still loved her. The tenderness with which he said the word *love* threw the interviewer off guard; unable to come up with a question, she moved on to commentary from a lawyer in the studio. The lawyer explained that, according to our democratic constitution, a person could not be prohibited from painting in the street, in a public space, as long as he didn't impede movement: "It's a fundamental right of the citizenry." When the painter refused to leave, the restaurant owner objected to what she called "the invasion of my psychological space" and threatened him with lawsuits and psychiatric hospitals.

But the young painter stayed there, day after day, delicately setting down every detail of the restaurant with those wide, long-lashed eyes of his that appear in close-up on the television screen. At first, he would wait for her to close the restaurant, at around midnight, and offer her the paintings he'd done that day. She would rip them up and then leave. Now, he finishes before closing time; he rolls up the canvases nice and slowly, puts them in his car, and waits in the dark to watch her leave. Only then does he head off in the opposite direction. She smokes a lot, has an irritated gait, perhaps because of her too-high heels or her clingy skirts; she's short and looks to be about fifty years old, with a tired face.

Sometimes the people who come out of the restaurant want to buy one of the paintings, but he shakes his head and insists the canvases aren't for sale. The subject is always the same, but none of the canvases are the same; the painter captures the unique light of every time of day, the rain, the springtime sun on the women's hair, the brown leaves of summer, the parties and the slow times at the restaurant.

One day I took Camila to see the show up close. "As paintings, they're nothing interesting," she said. "Naïve neorealism. Even my father could have done better." It made me too sad to respond. All I could have said was that in her father's time, painting had been something that actually obliterated the fleeting notion of interesting. It's just as well I didn't say that, because it wasn't even true. I saved myself another pointless fight about "my time"; in speaking in such terms, one always perpetrates injustices, most of all against one's own memories. In my time painting was a dying art, though that wasn't so obvious in Portugal because we had never been a colorful country. It doesn't seem like such a big deal to me. Most likely, everything's already been painted before; the Vermeers and Rembrandts and Gauguins and Picassos had their time, and now we're performing their funeral rites through reproductions, collages, quotations that mourn them, through the keening of a nostalgia that is sometimes insulting, as absence is a place of wreckage.

Death sells more and better than life does; television proves that, and here at the beginning of the final decade of the twentieth century, the visual arts sell for the exorbitant price of their own death rattle. Every day there are writers, journalists, children, and computer technicians declaring the death of literature, explaining that it's too late, that screens will replace paper through the power of synthesis and limitless options. Things can't really be that bad—I see no signs of a terminal condition. Movies feed on books; in the peace and quiet of books, dreams and ideas continue to resist the hegemony of mobs; Camila tells me that even in places like Mozambique, where hunger rules people's souls, books are treasured and quarreled over. But they're cheap too—writers complain that nobody values the work of writing; they compare the grants and subsidies the government gives to visual artists, the astronomical values ascribed to their works, and declare themselves at death's door. "Pieces, Grandma. Nobody talks about 'works' of art these days. The notion of a painting or sculpture is passé; it's been dismantled and upcycled. People talk about 'pieces' now," Natália explains.

And so: we are reduced to squabbling over the pieces; that's why arte povera makes people so rich. Indeed, the history of art demonstrates that profits accrue in tribute to bereavement. Most likely, photographs and cinema and computers will completely replace painting and sculpture in the end. Most likely, great painting, like great music, no longer endures in this world. Instead of artists, we have specialists in visual communication, dressed by specialists in fashion, who fill the museums with broken plates, soup cans, and heaped-up television sets.

It's likely that only the young painter of neo-naïve canvases remains, there in front of the restaurant. But that doesn't matter, because it's not painting that he's interested in.

I stopped counting the days and nights. I think I always existed outside the succession of seasons and years, fleeing from the way life leaves one laid bare, its dense wastefulness. I awoke this morning with

Josefa's rusty voice repeating to me, "Leaving already, are you? Don't tell me you've got a dinner, sweetheart." Illness stripped her of the diplomatic, baroque sense of ceremony with which she'd stifled her explosive personality. Intubated, immobile, without teeth to smile or hinder her words, she abandoned her role as a seductress and relieved her sorrows by clearing them away, clumps of dried mud on the indifference of those she loved most. Only then did I realize the extent to which she, who seemed so free, depended on half a dozen deep, obsessive friendships.

"I never told you I had *a* dinner, Jenny. I always told you everything. I'd say, I'm going to have dinner with Zé, or the Mouras, or the girls from the association, or something like that. I was an idiot. You're always on the defensive: I have a dinner. I have a lunch. I can't tomorrow, I have a prior commitment. Really, Jenny, I'm amazed you have time to come see me at all. Must be you want to make sure I'm about to croak. Don't worry, tiresome Josefa won't be spoiling your comfortable life anymore." And so, quite late in life, I discovered a capacity for hurt, lashing and silent, made of thousands of little electric shocks that propel people along the tracks of proper social lethargy. It was no use telling Josefa it wasn't true, that I'd never trade her for any comfort, that my brevity was merely a sign of respect and humility; it had never occurred to me that my comings and goings—which were so few and so pointless—might interest her. It was no use: with the curtains of explanation pulled aside, her ardor continued to glow, intact, against the pallor of my lassitude. It was no use because Josefa really existed only on the secondary stages of my life, light comedy that served as an occasional distraction from the central drama that was you, António. I grasped Josefa's skinny, doomed hand and knew that in her place, in the deterioration that life offers us as a taste of our fate so we'll off-load our mortality onto the backs of those who survive us, I would have blamed you.

You abandoned me when you placed a motherless child in my arms. I don't know how many nights I spent futilely singing to her, pacing the vast room, lined with cold and mirrors, where you moved me so you wouldn't have to hear her cry. When I was a little girl, I used to tiptoe past the door of that empty room to avoid waking the ghosts that surely dwelled there. Despite my terror, I wasn't brave enough to defy your orders; I convinced myself that you were the victim and that yours were the only tears that burned.

I'd never learned to take care of a child. I could have handed her over to the maids, but I wanted to keep her as a personal trophy. It was not thanks to the broad generosity of my purported maternal instinct that people—you foremost among them—believed I embodied the best of womanhood. It was to make you jealous. To show you that Pedro didn't belong solely to you, that I was bound to him too. And so that you would admire the elegance and facility with which I raised a little girl. But you didn't even notice: you came to love Camila because of the charms she and Pedro shared, and I became superfluous, mere decoration.

I was jealous of her, but there was no turning back; I needed Camila the way I needed air to breathe. I fell head over heels for her during those difficult first months, there in the haunted room. I felt like Camila's daughter because she had given me the strength to face the menacing spirits in the mirror room. Camila liked me better than anything or anyone else, which was an intoxicating novelty. I'd never occupied that place in anyone's heart. She gave me security, discipline, joy, reality. She taught me; I had only to let myself be guided by her needs. I did not let myself be moved by the folds of her plump little body or the dimples of her smile. That child never seemed vulnerable; when I took her in, I felt that I was submitting to her, and a few days later, when you banished the two of us to that remote room, António, I felt that you were delivering me into her hands, the way a father turns a daughter over to her groom.

Danielle promised to write, but fate prevented her from keeping that promise. Pedro said she didn't like to write, and you were delighted, António. You remarked on the weakness of women's memories, how they forget about lovers and children as they might a pair of gloves carelessly left on a garden bench. I thought I'd be able to forget, that old age's great triumph would be the irrelevance of suffering, but after visiting Josefa in her final days, I gave up that notion. When Danielle brought us Camila, I asked her, "How did you seduce Pedro?" I don't know how I managed to ask her, out of the blue, just like that. There was something about her that immediately inspired trust; maybe it was the shadow of her impending tragedy and the abrupt joy that emanated from her. She laughed, grasped my hands, and whispered, "I didn't seduce him, *ma chérie*. I just grabbed him, the way men have always done with women. It works for them, so why shouldn't it work for us? It's strange—I grabbed him, and now I'm letting him go, with my own daughter in his arms. God knows I never wanted to be such a cliché. I never imagined history could be turned upside down with such sarcastic precision. *C'est la vie.*"

I always loved you for the pleasure it gave me to see you living. I was horrified by the idea of constricting someone's movements, of creating a fixed orbit of attraction. You and I were always quite different that way. We were both passionate, but for me passion had to be the ecstasy of freedom. Perhaps it is more honest to say that, at bottom, I didn't believe it possible to catch and hold someone. I still don't. It is always a futile humiliation. Your persistent attempts to control Pedro's comings and goings did not prevent Camila's birth; I think they even hastened it. It was only through many dozens of insignificant infidelities that Pedro managed to remain faithfully by your side for a lifetime. The more you suffocated him with surveillance, weeping, and recriminations, the more he sought out other bodies that allowed him to return, safe and sound, to you. The intimate spectacle of your life together spooled out exclusively for me.

I realize now that no friend was ever truly real for me—not even Josefa, and so I wounded her unawares. I became so accustomed to being a spectator that any attempt at closeness struck me as superfluous. I offered Josefa the excuses of largely nonexistent lunches and dinners so as not to have to give up my spot in the front row. In addition, she had many friends and acquaintances and made an enormous effort to maintain a maximum of social relationships in a simultaneous gentle glow, which allowed me to avoid confronting that eagerness to survive, which diminished her so much in my eyes. I sometimes thought Josefa despised Veleno because she recognized in him some of her greatest frailties.

The only things I forget are the ones that give order and continuity to life. More and more often now I forget to eat, to sleep. I sometimes forget to bathe and get dressed; a few days ago I went down to the corner bakery in my nightgown, robe, and slippers. If not for people's laughter, I wouldn't have noticed. I felt the cold slice my legs as I left the house, but it didn't occur to me to bundle up. Quite the contrary: I focused on courageously facing the violence of nature. I didn't even look down. Life is an endless collection of testimonies. We need to be observed, both in victory and in failure; we need to be paid attention to. I was always afraid of being trapped by others' gazes, of having to rely on someone's testimony. I think I wouldn't be able to bear the disillusionment that would drive me toward a world that is too real, like in a television documentary. I am a product of the age of words. I learned to make words slide along my body, slowly, like leaves falling in autumn. But now I feel them in their own lairs, separate from me, boring into my head and issuing from my mouth as if nobody had uttered them and they had been born and died all on their own. Natália recently scolded me because apparently I said to her, "Leaving already, are you? Don't tell me you've got a dinner. Tiresome Jenny is always spoiling your comfortable life, isn't she, sweetheart?"

10

I am lying on the grass, eating bread with sugar, hiding from my mother. She says if I keep eating sugar my teeth are going to fall out and I'll get fat, and then I'll never find a husband. But I'd rather spend my whole life like this, lying on the grass, feeling the weight of my body pressing into the damp earth, than find a husband who'll go off and die in the war, like my father did.

Besides, I have really pretty fingernails, and men like fingernails too. Whenever her boyfriend comes to see her at the gate, Dores goes to my mother's dressing table to steal a little bit of red polish, and she paints her nails very carefully, pushing down the skin on her fingers and leaving the white half-moons clearly visible. Today I made her paint mine too, otherwise I'd go tell my mother everything. Rosário shakes her head and says men who get excited about red lacquered nails must be devils, never good men. But Rosário is never going to get married; she's got a limp from where her father beat her. I am eight years old; the bed in the haunted room is full of apples ripening in the dark to make preserves; my skinny braids smell like the mixture of fresh eggs and lemon that Rosário uses to wash my hair.

My mother's clouded face visits me now with increasing regularity, promising me death by excessive lucidity. Moments of an unfamiliar childhood memory come back to me. I'm eight again, lying on the grass, but it doesn't give way beneath my girlish weight as obediently as I remember—the earth is hard, its odor intense; my bones hurt; the sun scrapes my eyes, suffocates my chest. And you laugh at me, António—you kiss my mother on the mouth and the two of you laugh at me. I can't allow myself the luxury of crying; the more I cry, the louder your ringing laughter echoes.

Camila hired a spy to live with me, a spy who stole china and towels and raided my pantry. This spy would reprimand me when she found me drinking my whiskey, and she ate my jams, poisoned my broth, snooped in my journals, talked about me behind my back. I caught her conspiring with the other women on the street and fired her. I got rid of her before Camila had me committed thanks to the spy's connivances. Camila is embarrassed by me; when she found me in the corner bakery, she stripped off her jacket and covered my head with it. As if I weren't a thousand times prettier than she is. Especially now. Back when she was a hippie she would wear full lace skirts, quite modest, or richly colored corduroys, and lots of flowers. Now she goes around in polyester miniskirts, her bony knees protruding like duck legs over the grim combat boots she wears no matter the occasion— but it's she who's embarrassed by me. She punishes me, takes away my drinks, as if I were the daughter here. I bore her. She asks me the same trivial things over and over, and all she talks about is other people's diseases, ailments, and misfortunes. Ever since I told her she'd be better off doing something creative, that taking photographs is child's play—just a question of having a high-quality camera—she's stopped speaking to me. When she visits it's like she's performing some sort of penance, and on top of that she drinks the spirits she won't let me have.

Even books irritate me—I open them and the words hide from me, dissolving into a river of black ink that reminds me that I'm alone, that in the end I have nobody, that perhaps I've never actually had anybody to whom I could give all my love. It gets harder and harder to write. I have nothing to do but think. And thinking starts to gnaw away at the candy house of my life. And beneath that house's chocolate floorboards is a mound of unrecognizable decomposing corpses that reach out their arms to grab me and slowly drain me of my voice.

There's no point in speaking anyway. Words distance us from the truth, push us toward a reality in which we cannot grasp the truth of things. "Turn on the TV, Grandma. Why don't you watch TV?" Natália asks, and I reply that there's nothing to see on the boob tube. "But you can't spend all day staring at your fingernails, Grandma!" Of course I can: they're flexible, gleaming, pink as they were when I was a girl, when I didn't know how to paint them. And nobody knows how to paint nails anymore; not even manicurists know how to emphasize the outline of the lunule. "There's no time for that nonsense, Grandma."

It's true, Natália, there's no time. We're all going to die, but nobody has time to do anything thoroughly, from beginning to end. Love, for example. You didn't have time for it—you married a man you didn't love so as not to waste time being happy. The houses you design don't have time either: made of glass and aluminum, they'll last a decade or two, begin to rust, be destroyed to make way for other more modern, cheaper structures. The only thing you like that's made of stone and old wood is me. You conspire against me just like your mother does, stealing my cakes and cutwork embroidery, but you cover me with kisses and never get angry with me.

I like your spiraling laughter, your eyes that are always looking toward the joy of things. They remind me of my life. You nag me about imagining the world my own way, scorning realities, but you do the same thing, darling Natália. You create ideal people from real contours. You feed the love that Manuel Almada had for me. You prolong me. Like me, you fear intimacy, which comforts men and unsettles women. You say, "My God, I waste so much time trying to make people like me that I don't have time to do anything important." You inherited my principle of weighing priorities, even if you didn't really know it. And soon I, too, will no longer know. That's why it's so hard for me when you come; that's why I have such a hard time when you leave.

Yes, I am certain I'm going to go mad again. And I know that this time I won't get better. I'm starting to hear voices, and I can't concentrate. Panic grips me. I feel my body surging with thick blood that will not drain away. I cut my skin, and it doesn't flow out. This must be death, the disappearance of dreams. I can barely hear you, António; I hear shards of sentences, strangers threatening to lock me in a wine cellar with a knot of old women who perpetually stink of urine, constant banging, a drill screeching all day long inside my head. I can't remember your face, my love—I go out into the street and recognize you in every man, which must mean I'm irretrievably forgetting you. But I long for you more urgently every day; I wake up in the middle of the night to the sensation of your breath, your fingers exploring inside my body, hurting me, taking me to heaven.

Camila's Album

*"One can only raise happiness on a foundation of despair.
I think I will be able to start building."*

—*Marguerite Yourcenar*

1

Danielle

Summer 1941

My mother is smiling and her eyes are two slits of light; she's awash in a flood of sunshine that makes her too physical, almost evanescent. Behind her are the shadows of the trees on Avenida da Liberdade, a hurrying man with a briefcase in his hand, two blurry kids, a ball hovering in the air, the blotch of the Glória Funicular. Her dress is light-colored with a full skirt, sleeveless. Her plump arms are spread wide, like she's about to hug somebody. Or like she's dancing, all by herself, in the middle of the street. She's wearing the pearl necklace and the earrings she left me as part of my inheritance. In this photograph I didn't even exist yet. Or maybe I'd just been born inside her.

I like thinking that it's me, deep within her, who's making her smile like that. It's strange, because I don't like smiles. I saw too many of them during the interrogations. First they smiled at me with promises: good jobs, gallery exhibits, photography jaunts all around the world. Then they got annoyed and started smiling at me with threats: they were going to arrest my father, Tó Zé, or Jenny, or they were going to have to treat me badly. I answered their smiles with laughter, not so much to insult them as to shield myself from the idea of the bad things they could do to me. Later, I kept laughing to keep from hearing the cries coming from the other cells, telling myself it wasn't real, it was just them screaming on the other side of the wall to terrorize me.

They said that Glória Veleno had told them everything, that they knew I was a communist but were prepared to pardon me. All I had to do was collaborate—everybody makes mistakes when they're young. All I had to do was give them some names and sign some papers. I knew Glória hadn't told them anything. Back then I harbored absolute certainties. Heroism was merely a natural consequence of those certainties. I didn't even need to muster courage; my best friend's dark eyes, I was convinced, could never be clouded by betrayal. Ultimately, it was a question of aesthetics. Photography showed me that a truth could be captured forever. Afterward, when the truth ceased to exist outside of the stillness of images, I became obsessed with taking photographs.

Glória was my doppelganger—maybe that's why I took so few photos of her. She had the same feelings as me, which dwelled in a heart identical to mine, and at the same time she had many things that were out of my reach. She was fast. She was pretty. She had a gift for words. Jenny told me once, "You're passionate about friendship the way I'm passionate about love, darling. I don't know which is more tragic." I must have been about eighteen, and I spent all my time consoling Glória, who was always falling hopelessly in love with insensitive men. "Promise me that if I die and you happen to go to my funeral, you won't let him into the cemetery. I don't want him there. Promise." I'd promise, kiss her teary cheeks, and feign outrage. Happen to go? If I happened to go to her funeral? I would stay with her till the end of time.

But Glória would quickly console herself. Or perhaps she was actually inconsolable. She covered up one sorrow with another—men paraded into her life one after the other, like shovelfuls of dirt into a bottomless pit. She'd always say, "I don't know what I'd do without you. Nothing is that bad as long as you exist." And I reinforced that confidence in our unshakable friendship. Love, it seemed to me then, was a childish emotion, capricious, impalpable as the south wind. I liked it when Glória fell in love only to confirm that I was the one enduring love in her life. And the two of us had lots of fun. We used to go to ice hockey matches all by ourselves. Or we'd hang out in her room, jumping on the bed, listening to the stories on the radio.

She once ended it with a boyfriend because he didn't want her hanging around with somebody like me. What I called simplicity, many others called slovenliness: as I saw it, wasting time doing up one's eyes, painting one's nails, and curling one's hair was an appalling acquiescence to patriarchal oppression. I'd just finished reading *Le Deuxiéme Sexe* and was determined to make sure nobody ever again told me my ideas were "bizarre" or "feminine." I dressed in black, gray, or brown and wore flat lace-up shoes. Even Josefa, Jenny's friend who'd lent me the book, thought I was going overboard. But the truth was I loved the startled look on people's faces when I walked by holding Glória's hand: her with vibrant red hair, statuesque, wearing high heels and pink dresses, her black eyes flecked with green, and me, skinny, dusky, narrow, abstemious, dark. Like day and night, Jenny used to say.

It's funny: I find it impossible to think of Jenny as my mother when I'm looking at this photo of Danielle, my birth mother.

In this family album, hers is the only image I did not create. I have been haunted by the silence of her laughter ever since childhood. I never really heard my mother's voice—I think that's why I chose to become a photographer. Everything she ever told me is contained in this rectangle of light; Lisbon is a splotch of shadows behind my luminous mother and her timeless laugh. Her laughter guided me through the delirium of my days of torture. There were times, on those nights when they kept me sleepless on my feet, when the joy of Glória's black eyes evaporated and only my mother caressed me. I was no longer listening to what they said; I was convinced they were speaking German and we were in a frost-covered concentration camp, so there was no point in trying to say anything. Carlos Bonito circled around me with a lamp that pinned me. I looked down at the floor, and he hit me; his voice grew softer, transporting me to the amber-suspended time of our shared childhood, and I burst out laughing as I saw that his feet were growing wider and becoming covered with scales, he looked like a crocodile struggling to walk upright, and his upper limbs started to probe me, to examine my whole body, outside and in, impatient to steal whatever they could not manage to grab. There was nothing true about Carlos Bonito, so he didn't exist.

Afterward, I discovered that those days of torture had been useful for reassessing my photographic approach. I was no longer fascinated by transparencies, by superimpositions, and instead seized on the kind of immediate beauty that stops you short. I also stopped believing in the party, which abandoned those who were arrested during the first protest, at the peak of their youth. I suppose I flung myself onto the front lines of danger out of disillusionment. The men of the party were patronizing to their female comrades, wanting them to remain chaste and devoted in the rearguard of the men's masculine activities, cooking and mending trousers in the domestic shadows of the underground. Glória would say, "I'll always stand with you, but I'm not going to give up wearing makeup out of political conviction. I don't believe in that. I think Salazar's awful—isn't that enough?" In the end, the party was not the resistance, and I was unable to redeem Danielle's death. All I could do was love her, and Jenny said that was the only power that could prevent her from being forgotten.

Nobody told me my father never loved the plump Jewess I saw bestowing the last of her laughter upon Lisbon. But I knew. Everything I know about Danielle I learned from Jenny. My father would just shrug and say, with curt embarrassment, that everything had happened really fast and a long time ago. It was he who took this photo of her, and it's in contrast to his indifference that she shines so radiantly. It was an impromptu snapshot, which is evident in the faint blurring of the image, the uncentered subject, the clumsy cropping of the legs just above the ankle. And in her laughter, her eyes squeezed nearly shut, happy apart from him, despite him.

2

Eduardo

Autumn 1962

"I'm going to die now, and you'll never forget me." He lay down on a bed of dry leaves, settled his bent arms next to his head the way children do when they're going to sleep, turned his neck to his left, and closed his eyes. That's when I took the shot. It was the only photo that allowed me to hang on to dead Eduardo, captured half a year before his death. The light filtered by the trees in the Monserrate gardens marks his face with splotches of smooth wax. It looks as if he stopped breathing just a moment earlier and is already looking down, from some higher place, at that serene body that used to be his, amazed at its serenity. He had no right to posthumous contemplations, that slim, boyish body from which I first discovered love. He disappeared from the face of the earth, disintegrated into black ashes on the sand, devoured by a bolt of lightning before my eyes.

It was the first warm day of spring. At five o'clock, Eduardo came by the newspaper to steal me away: "Let's get out of here, the sun is calling." In reality, the sun was barely peeking out, warming up the fog that cloaked the sky, and I had a lot of work to do. Tomorrow, I pleaded. "We don't know that we'll still be here tomorrow," he answered.

He was euphoric. At first I thought it was because of the rehearsals for a new play of his, an adaptation of Virginia Woolf's *The Waves* set in the midst of an unidentified war, in which four lost children—two white and two black—grew up, oblivious, in an endless and seemingly illogical conversation. But it became clear there was little chance the piece might one day be performed. There wasn't any money, and it was quite likely, however much the war remained unidentified and the language metaphorical, that the play wouldn't be authorized by the regime. Nevertheless, they rehearsed every day for hours at a stretch. Eduardo pretended the rehearsals were real performances. He knew he'd have to leave the country soon—he was about to be called to the real war, in Africa.

He was planning to desert. He had long arguments about it with his mother, a widow with nobody else in the world besides her one son, whom she doted on. She insisted she'd much rather see Eduardo as a dead hero than a living deserter: "I'm ashamed to have given birth to a man who refuses to defend our homeland with his life. You dishonor me. If I could, I'd go fight for what's ours myself. Your attitude is an affront to God, the Portuguese nation, and your father's memory." Eduardo responded with the Church's first commandment—"Thou shalt not kill"—which nearly put his mother into a state of shock. After that bolt of lightning obliterated him, she no longer accepted me there at the house, didn't even speak to me. She'd liked me in the early days. I think she interpreted my ascetic fashion sense as modesty. Sometimes she'd suggest, with a magnanimous smile, that I was neglecting my beauty: "You have such pretty eyes, it wouldn't hurt to put a little effort into them. Have you tried wearing eyeliner? And don't take this the wrong way, but if you wore more cheerful colors and some high heels, you'd look stunning." I would smile, biting my lips to keep from laughing, but Eduardo wasn't one to let anything go: "She doesn't want to be stunning, Mother. She has other goals in life. That's why I like her." Eventually, Eduardo's mother started commenting that her son had gotten grumpier ever since he'd fallen in love with me. And then one morning she came into his bedroom and found us sleeping naked in each other's arms. After that, Eduardo stayed at my house every other day. He felt too guilty to abandon his mother altogether, and she, for her part, began to suffer an ongoing series of maladies. Jenny pretended not to notice that Eduardo was spending nights in my room, offering him breakfast as if he'd just arrived. My father and Uncle Tó Zé didn't notice a thing; they always went to bed late, generally heading out to the casino at eleven at night and returning at daybreak. They were clearly taken with each other, but at the time I didn't want to think about what that fascination might mean. I needed to think of myself as having a father, however tenuous the notion might have been. Even so, when I fell for Eduardo I felt something very akin to the pulverizing energy that emanated from my father and Tó Zé. They loved Eduardo because he'd managed to get me to laugh again, and they were grateful to him for helping me overcome my resistance to the physical expression of affection.

When I first came back from prison, I couldn't stand having people touch me, not even a pat on the head. Though he'd never been incarcerated, Eduardo understood the terror in my eyes from the very start. One day when the two of us were walking along the riverbank, he looked at me, interrupting a conversation about cameras, and said, "I'm completely in love with you. It's all I can think about. I'd really like it if you'd at least give me your hand." And so I was the one to take the initiative in that first slow, overwhelming caress of his fingers. From that point on we couldn't be close to each other without touching. Glória used to tease me, her tenderness tinged with sadness: "So it turns out love is more contagious than friendship after all, huh? Not even the sisterhood of the Beauvoirian nuns can escape it."

The truth is, there's nothing so cruel as true love. We spend entire lifetimes tracking down suspects, questioning witnesses. Everybody knows it has happened, but nobody's seen it. Nobody can describe its face. It is most likely to attack distracted people or during distracted hours, without the knowledge or consent of that comfortable human device we call reason. And it attacks with a vengeance. It upends the serene order of this world, in which people are always running over each other in pursuit of another car, an additional room, a promotion. In the light of my love for Eduardo, Glória's flings seemed as pathetic as her enormous collection of slinky dresses.

Passion upsets the world's economy; it is success's only insolvency. The more you lose, the more you gain. "I can't give you anything," we'd tell each other, having already given each other everything. No thief could steal the pain of being unable to inhabit our own other halves outside of space and time. Academics open parentheses and elucidate this miracle, intense and fleeting, untreatable as a coronary flu, dwelling on the opposite shore from love, quiet, laborious, edifying, clear, "permanently under construction." With Eduardo I didn't need to construct anything. I would have gone off with him to war or into exile, without hesitating, leaving behind everything I loved. His scintillating body was emerging from the waves and I was just grabbing the camera to fix him in place once more when the bolt of lightning struck him and the world collapsed around me. I don't remember what happened afterward. I have retained only his mother's accusation, her dry eyes as she grasped my hands that sought the flesh of her flesh: "It's your fault. God carried him off to hell, and it's all your fault."

I miss the heat of my heart. I thought it was an inborn gift, an inexhaustible grace; nothing gave me more pleasure than sharing that ardor; no glory can compare to the intoxicating sensation of bringing another person back to life. Now, in Africa, I awake at first light with my body boiling and my heart brimming over with ice. As soon as I open my eyes, the procession of graves begins to file before me, the stones slowly rising, one after another, in a welcoming ceremony. I search for the shadow of a corpse in each grave, but as I approach, the stone closes up again, revealed only by a blade of cold air. The viscera that warmed the world become a saturated cemetery where the dead amass in a unified bulk, feeding on the earth rather than dissolving into it.

I came to Africa in search of a place to bury this death that is suffocating me with its weight, but I'm afraid it's too late; the music of suffering is so repetitive that after a while, all of the things that used to torment us meld together, forming a firmament of despair that covers us like a dome.

3

Xavier, Xai-Xai Beach

November 1964

I didn't like this photograph when the two of us first looked at it. Xavier's head was in front of a fishing boat, which formed a bizarre sort of hat. And the sunlight had created harsh shadows. But Xavier looked at me and said, "You know, baby, you know too much. You need to learn to unknow some things so life doesn't seem so unpleasant. This photo portrays the face of a happy man. That's not an easy thing to capture on film." The night after the photo was taken we slept together for the first time. The little hotel was on the beach; there were two palm trees practically invading the room's little porch, and then the sea. Xavier had come to visit a cousin of his by marriage and help him build a house. He didn't have much family left. His first two children had died of cholera. His wife was living with her mother in Feitor Praça, a village farther inland.

After three months in Lourenço Marques, I felt suffocated, hemmed in on all sides by resentful women who kept themselves busy organizing pathetic receptions where they played at military hierarchies with the utmost seriousness. The captain's wife paid tribute to the lieutenant colonel's wife, the brigadier's wife to the general's, and beneath the cozy facade of intimate conversation about children, ill-nesses, diets, and tedium, there were strict codes of dress and language to be followed.

I had come to Mozambique to report on the drama unfolding there. My assignment was to show continental Portugal our soldiers' great generosity in their civilizing mission.

There didn't appear to be a way to go any deeper than the official visits to immaculate barracks on the city outskirts, where neat platoons performed meticulous circus acts. Half a dozen black soldiers gave the white troops a little pizzazz, singing the Portuguese national anthem—"Brave, immooooortal nation!"—at the top of their lungs. I called the editor-in-chief every day, pleading with him to arrange a guide to take me to the country's interior. He would laugh and tell me not to push myself, to enjoy the sun and the beaches; if I did the story I was looking to do, he said, it was just going to make more problems for him, and the photos could never be published anyway. Finally, I managed to join up with some troops who were traveling south. There'd been reports of skirmishes in the Xai-Xai district. I wandered the bush with the soldiers during the day. They organized daily sweeps of several square kilometers, supposedly to prevent ambushes. In reality, though, whenever they caught a whiff of an indigenous village, they prudently re-treated. "We must exercise our bodies and maintain peace," the official repeated. I began to suspect they'd brought me along just so I'd give up and discard my fantasies of bloody combat. After a week they deemed the area pacified and decided to go unwind for a few days at the beach. It was there that I met the man who would be my daughter's father.

Xavier was a member of FRELIMO, the Mozambique Liberation Front, and had participated in the attack on the Mueda air base, which had sparked the armed conflict, in retaliation for the massacre there four years earlier. At first he avoided me, taking me for the wife of a Portuguese soldier. But one day, hearing the shutter go off as I aimed my camera at him, he dropped his shovel and came up to me in a fury.

"Give me that roll of film, ma'am. If you don't hand it over, I'm going to have to take it from you, and I'm not one for taking things from women." Everything happened really quickly.

Time in Africa is like space in Africa: so vast that you don't even notice it. The sun suddenly falls and then effortlessly rises to its zenith in the sky. Intensity replaced hours just as truth replaced seduction. Xavier trusted me from the very beginning. I looked him in the eye and told him, "I'm not trying to do anything to hurt you. This photo is just for me." And he believed me. He leaned closer, at a distance smaller than that of time and space, and asked, with a surprised smile, "Then what use is that camera, ma'am? Are your eyes forgetful—are they sick?" "No," I replied. "Photos are the only proof I exist." He started laughing and said I had caught Europe's disease, which was communicated through European books. "It's the disease of thinking, ma'am. If you weren't so white, I'd try to cure you of it." I found myself saying that I wasn't white, but Jewish, that my mother had been killed by the whitest of the white, and that I'd come to Africa to save myself from that whiteness. "I don't know about saving yourself, ma'am. Only the witch doctor in my village can do that. Or the party, if the gods are willing. But first we have to bury the vanity of suffering. And the vanity of thought, which is harder to pull off."

Even so, it was only after we'd slept together that he told me about the Mozambique Liberation Front, Eduardo Mondlane, and the Mueda Massacre. He refused to let me accompany him into the interior, where the guerrilla fighting was intensifying: it was dangerous and not allowed. He promised to come looking for me in Lourenço Marques in a month. "I'll find you. Letters? What for? Words won't put my body on top of yours. I'll be back soon."

Maybe you couldn't call what I felt for Xavier "love." When we were apart, I didn't feel that icy blade that cleaves a path into lovers' consciousness once night falls. As long as I believed in Xavier's life, my days could begin and end without him. Things were never like that with Eduardo: it was impossible for me to think that a whole day of my life might drain away without him. With Xavier, I simply stopped thinking. I focused on listening to the blood in my body until its voice was more powerful than the blood-parching silence of the dead. That's how I created Natália. My daughter was sired by Africa more than by Xavier. That's how he wanted it: the girl inheriting the continent's vastness rather than one man's tragic story. For Xavier, tragedy was merely proof of life's urgency. "Why bother with all those little words, baby?" he used to say. "Love, passion, sex, affection . . . it's all just emotion—why block the heavens' light with all those paper clouds?"

Xavier cleansed the guilt and remorse from my body, offering me the innocence of a pleasure that predated the original sin of melancholy. His smooth black skin wrapped around me like the very first night the world ever saw, striving to iron out the creases of my memory, to bring my senses back to life.

I returned to the capital city with the Portuguese soldiers a few days after Xavier left for the interior. There were four casualties when one of the jeeps ran over a mine. I vomited the whole way back. By the time I got to Lourenço Marques, I knew I was pregnant. Two months later, Xavier hadn't returned. I returned to Xai-Xai with this photo. It's the only photo I have of him. The first one, the one he didn't want me to take, came out completely underexposed. In fact, when I developed the rolls from Xai-Xai, they were pretty much unsalvageable, full of inexplicable scratches, blotches, and blurring. From Xai-Xai, I headed to the interior, went all around Feitor Praça, but everybody scurried away when they saw what I was doing and refused to identify him. Finally, I managed to get a proud-eyed woman to confirm Xavier Sandramo had been captured by soldiers. She told me his head had appeared a few days later, impaled on a pike in front of the Feitor Praça school.

4

Decoration Ceremony, Terreiro do Paço
Lisbon, June 10, 1966

"Honor the Fatherland, for the Fatherland beholds you." With these words, the rector of the University of Mozambique closes his speech before more than four thousand parading soldiers. After that, President Américo Tomás starts giving out medals. One recipient is a corporal who managed to ignore the blood gushing from one of his eyes, pinned down by machine-gun fire, with the bulk of his fellow soldiers lying dead around him, and continued to fire on the attackers until the final victory. Another is a middle-aged peasant with a look of resignation on his face, the father of a stretcher bearer who continued to aid the wounded and shoot at the enemy until he became a lake of blood.

And when a two-year-old boy, sitting on the lap of his widowed and weeping mother, receives the medal awarded to the father he no longer has, two delicate tears trickle down Salazar's face. "Go on, take the shot!" Glória says. "Salazar's crying!" I see the way the light glimmers on the tears and bring the lie produced by this amplification of the truth into focus. I see, I focus, and I freeze there, my finger hovering over that moment in which the framing of eternity will be decided. "Take the photo, you twit! Stop screwing around. If you don't, I'll tell the story anyway. I'll make the stones sob with the poignancy of Boots's tears, and I'll throw you under the bus, say you didn't manage to get the shot." The outlines of the image float before my camera. It will appear on a magazine cover—many magazine covers, even. The foreign press will snap up this lucky take. Fame, prizes, consecration—I can have it all if I just zoom in on the old dictator's stirring face. But how can I underwrite a dictator's emotion? How can I accede to using his tears to conceal those that the young men he sent off to die can no longer shed?

"Take it, you twit," Glória repeats, and despite the tumult of immensely serious ideas barraging me, I start thinking this absolutely frivolous, completely tangential thing: how funny, Glória's polite manners are merely strung up on delicate wires, a picture-perfect facade. And this secondary thought obsessively overtakes all others; Glória's voice becomes deafening, bizarre, it hurts my ears, my fingers shake, and the photo is taken without my even meaning to, in perfect focus.

In the darkroom I'm struck by the authenticity of the emotion in the lonely old man's eyes. But what is authentic is not necessarily true. Truth resides in the smiling eyes of my black daughter. A reporter's mission, Glória used to say, is to relate what she sees, without ever seeking to be a guardian of the truth. The editor-in-chief is always reminding us that nobody's paying us to think: "Journalism isn't a school of philosophy, it's a school of life. If you're into fripperies and arts and crafts, you should just go home and sit embroidering by the window!" Then he laughs delightedly and adds, "See, I'm very patient with women—pretty much one in a million!" A reporter should be humble, accommodating to the evidence regarding your average, everyday man. A reporter's role is to give narrative consistency to the lives of simple, honorable men who abide by the laws of those who govern and work for their benefit. Truth is abstract; it cannot be seen. And a reporter presents concrete reality. In reality, Salazar wept on June 10, 1966, and I was the only one who photographed that reality. But how can I superimpose that real moment over the much more momentous reality of the nonexistent photos of Portugal's and Africa's dead?

This is one of my most beautiful photographs. It is a portrait, not of Salazar, but of aching solitude. The beauty of an intimate snapshot, timeless and therefore transcending all moral judgments. An open-ended symbol. It's the kind of image that can outlast its context, Glória would say, and appear decades later printed on T-shirts for the teen market. The power of solitude, the solitude of power. No matter where it comes from, the palpable ballast of the corpses serving as a plinth dissolves before the immortality of bronze. Hitler, Stalin, Fidel, Evita, Salazar—they become symbols and propagate themselves. I went to Glória and told her, "Bad luck. It was totally underexposed." It was the first time I ever lied to her.

5

Maurice Béjart's Roméo et Juliette

Coliseu dos Recreios, Lisbon, June 6, 1968

This time, I forgot about my principles. I operated my camera with passion, heart, licentiousness, impudence. I did close-ups of audience members' distorted faces, applause, tears. I did extremely long exposures. I used all the techniques I normally consider cheap tricks, and the cameras I use to escape from life offered me images of dancing that contain the truth of my life's dream.

This portrait of Maurice Béjart downstage at the end of the show, calling for a minute of silence for the murder of Robert Kennedy, "victim of violence and fascism," was never printed. I begged the editor to publish it, but without text, without captions, without context, as if it had sneaked into the middle of another random news story—in short, as a simple portrait of a man confronting the darkness of a world that was drowning in news of inaction. The editor laughed and said, "You never change! Not even to protect your daughter!" Protect my daughter? Illegitimate, half black, with an officially unknown dead man for a father. Nothing could protect her from that fate. Watching her grow up made me only angrier and more courageous. I showed her how to transform sadness into proud joy while she was still in kindergarten, when the kids used to yell "Blackie!" and the teachers pretended to comfort her with sweets and sympathetic murmurs.

That's why Maurice Béjart's work with the Ballet du XXe Siècle in the Coliseu, packed full of people hungering for freedom, was more important to me than the moon landing a year later. The impact on us of the Béjart performance was that of a sort of concentrated version of the May 1968 events in France. It wasn't easy to leave the country by that point, at least not for people like me who had a police record. We devised miniature revolutions during café conversations or on clandestine nights out.

We were militantly frivolous, especially the girls. We would perform the lugubrious erotic baptism of the males of our generation, which usually took place in whorehouses back then, by sleeping with them at the end of one of those interminable wee-hour conversations spent changing the world. I remember thinking sometimes, in the middle of the act, "If this is freedom, why do I feel so sad and upset? Why am I not rejecting this repellent breath?" But the dogmatic voice of my conscience immediately quashed these individualistic impulses, reminding me that ugly people, too, have a right to worldly pleasures and that I must not yield to the bourgeois paradigms of comparison, much less to the aesthetic strictures that had given rise to the horrors of Nazism.

I slept with men I didn't desire, and I wasn't even paid for it. Choice didn't suit a free young woman, mostly because young women who were truly free, like me—a single mother—were rare, and progressive-minded young men couldn't bear the idea of paying some down-on-her-luck stranger to satisfy their needs. To be healthy, satisfaction had to be accompanied by some sort of affection. Yet we were modern enough to know that sex is an animal instinct, inherently democratic, equally natural for both men and women—and the instinctive nature of the act suggested that there was no reason, among comrades, to establish a hierarchy of preferences or exclusivities. We repressed any hint of possession or jealousy, making a deliberate effort to consider all bodies equivalent.

In the social imagination, we came to be seen as the generation of lust and orgies. But nothing could be further from the repetitive monotony of those melancholy, silent, meaningless couplings. At the end of the night, each boy would take a girl by the hand and lead her to a room away from the meeting area. Or to their bedroom back at their parents' house, where they'd tiptoe in, carrying their shoes. It would always end the same way, before daybreak. They didn't talk dirty, because they respected women's dignity. We didn't exchange declarations of love, because rational intelligence prevailed. For the same reasons, we didn't tear each other's clothes off in a frenzy or wear alluring lingerie. Above all, we strove to distinguish the healthy deployment of sexuality from the perverse practices of alienation from pleasure that typify patriarchal capitalist society. My happiest memory from this period is the occasional complicity we girls shared some nights, telling secrets, giggling, and confiding in one another. We would take surreptitious revenge on the boys, comparing their performances to ward off the desolation of those dull encounters. They didn't talk to each other about us; they respected us—or, rather, they forgot about us.

More and more, Portugal seemed to me like a hidden house without books or music or any color other than the swallows in the eaves, deafeningly chirping, floating in the void of the sky. Lisbon's light, the summer tourists' sneakers and white shorts, only accentuated my longing for a world that was out of reach. That's why that one night with Maurice Béjart at the Coliseu was engraved on me as a rare moment of civilization, art, Europe. That's why, in the two entire rolls of film I shot, I boldly and unhesitatingly employed every photographic technique and freedom. For the first time it seemed to me that photography could be a sign of difference, the mark of a singular gaze, and not just a way of guaranteeing the posthumous persistence of reality.

During the epilogue of *Roméo et Juliette*, someone yelled out, "Make love, not war!" And afterward, on the now deserted stage, you could still hear voices clamoring over each other with news of wars around the world. By two in the morning, Béjart was already at the border, and the other performances had been canceled. An officious statement from Salazar claimed that the evening had involved "subversive exhortations directed at the youth and political theorizing entirely unrelated to the show itself. Given the struggle we must wage in defense of our national integrity, a foreign ballet company cannot be allowed to take inappropriate advantage of a Portuguese stage to undermine domestic objectives."

In that summer of 1968 I was arrested for nudism, along with five of my friends, on a deserted beach near Sesimbra. Women were wearing bikinis by then, but the big trend that summer was bathing suits that left your sides bare. Jenny used to say, looking at the fashion magazines with a dispirited air, "One of these days, clothing designers are going to end up out of work altogether." When I returned home after my father paid my bail and I'd spent three days in the Caxias jail, Jenny smiled, hugged and kissed me, and served me a glass of lemonade with some freshly baked chocolate cake. Before going to look for Natália, she smiled again and said, "Now that skin has been deemed a fabric, people can't get undressed anymore. So sad. It's the end of eroticism." Jenny never relied on logic to criticize people's attitudes or appearance. She preferred to destroy them through humor. She used to tell me, for instance, "With all of you wearing those Nehru shirts, I can't tell you and your boyfriends apart anymore. I sure hope you can!" With supremely moralistic innocence, I replied that our clothing signified a rejection of hostile urges.

At the end of the night that I saw *Roméo et Juliette*, I found myself with a man I barely knew draped around my shoulders, droning on about "spectacle, capitalism's true religion," and rebuking me for being so dazzled by the feeble, proto-bourgeois tale of the Verona lovers. I shed him at the streetcar door. In the desperation of thwarted sexual desire, he called me a "bourgeois cocktease." I continued on my own through the neon lights of Baixa, feeling for the first time that I was a free woman.

6

Glória Veleno at the Newspaper Offices

1970

I was always irritated by Glória in numerous trivial ways. But I put up a deliberate resistance to that irritation, and so drew closer to her in a bond that verged on religious devotion. In the end, possibly in rebellion against my father, my allegiance echoed Tó Zé's relationship with her father. People made fun of me when I attempted to justify it beyond any real possibility of justification. In private, for example, she would give heated speeches about tyranny, lifting her arms while railing against society's inaction in defending the most basic human rights. But when a document landed in front of her, requesting the very public act of a signature, she'd start quibbling over comma placement and push it away. Only when pressed urgently would she finally sign, but with her mother's last name: Gomes. "Well," she'd say, seeing the look of surprise on the face of anyone watching, "it's time women freed themselves from the patriarchal yoke." If someone asked her why she didn't also use her mother's name in her bylines, she had an explanation ready: "Look. It just doesn't sound good. A pen name is a pen name—it has nothing to do with a person's core beliefs. They're completely differ-ent registers." Glória was an expert at distinguishing between registers.

I remember once, when she signed in support of the feminist icons known as the Three Marias, Armanda, who was the feisty heart of our office, fed up with Glória's evasiveness, pulled out a pen and said, "That's great. Your homage to your mother is touching and all, but since nobody's actually going to know who this Glória Gomes person is, I'm going to put an asterisk here and refer them to your pen name down below." Glória went pale—to this day I'm not sure whether with rage or with terror. I never examined Glória's responses; I preferred photographing her, watching her live and preserving her in images of light that satisfied some need of mine. But on that occasion she said something I've never forgotten: "Being brazen about it doesn't seem like a good way of getting ahead." A vast silence fell around her, and Glória started stammering excuses: she could lose her job, and anyway what was the point, what good would the name of a mere journalist really do? Armanda scratched her name off the paper, and everybody turned their backs on her, leaving her alone there in the newspaper office. I felt disgust and pity for the both of us.

Women tended not to like Glória. They criticized her high heels, her skimpy clothing, her lavishly applied makeup, even her naturally red hair. They put up with my devotion to her, dismissing it as a childhood vice. I insisted that Glória grew on you, that she was a fervent soul who was unsettled and disoriented by the ambiguities of the world. They did not understand me, which only reinforced my need for her. Where other women saw an uninhibited seductress, I found a dissonant presence that gleamed amid the dull array of our eternally besieged ideals. I agreed with her more often than I was able to admit on matters such as women's liberation or the arbitrary valuing of emotions over political logic.

Contrary to popular belief, Glória's love life was as consistent as it was unsuccessful. Men were frightened by her exuberant sensuality at a time when girls were going androgynous, shedding their bras and hiding their forms under loose tunics. And they were even more frightened by the evident will to power that shone in her eyes, so different from the docile femininity of their utopian female comrades, who were willing to step aside to follow the masculine voices that would lead them to a marvelous tomorrow. Glória often fell in love with people, but she was never able to fall in love with an idea. She'd get halfway there and start picking it apart, then get lost, fail to fit the pieces together, and give up. She was impatient. She tended to fall in love with men linked to power, which seemed to me to be of a piece with her genetic attraction to success, but it was highly frowned upon by nearly all of our colleagues at the newspaper, who accepted only the success of the Left.

When I lost my job at the beginning of February 1974, Glória told me, "Sorry, but I have to think about myself first. It's a dog-eat-dog world. There's nothing I can do." She added that nothing would shake our friendship, a job was just a job, and she offered to loan me money. I had been fired for refusing to scale the wall at the home of a famous actress to take pictures of her furtive encounters with a prominent—and married—businessman. After Salazar's death, Marcello Caetano's so-called political spring had ruffled the pages of the newspapers, and the loosening of censorship seemed to demotivate our readers. The editor started getting nervous and talking about audiences, marketing, targets, and dividing up Portuguese society, which we'd previously considered to be split merely between the oppressors and the oppressed, into classes A, B, C, and D, according to scientific indicators of economic capacity and consumption. "What readers are looking for is spectacle, escape." And the great escape, the biggest fantasy of all, was debauchery in the private lives of the rich and powerful. "I'll give you the cover. That's how we'll bring down the regime, undermining it from within," he said. "It's about showing the rotten core of a society that's all facade, see?" I just shook my head. No, I didn't see. I replied that politics should be addressed through political means, and that journalists couldn't act like a secret police unit enforcing other people's morals, no matter who they were. He told me that a responsible professional couldn't refuse a task assigned by her boss, and that if I insisted on insubordination he'd be forced to fire me.

Glória listened to our entire conversation in silence. She'd left reporting to host an interior decorating program on television, and the editor had decided to utilize her fame back at the newspaper again by giving her a weekly column, Glória Days, which ran with a headshot. A name can determine a destiny, as Delfim Veleno well knew. "Don't you have anything to say?" I asked her when the editor stomped off and slammed the door. She turned her large black eyes toward me and said, "I really like you, Camila. You know that." I asked her if she would be willing to speak up on my behalf, and she said, "I can't get involved in that sort of thing. And I don't think there's any use. That's the way the world is." I picked up my cameras and left. I never spoke to her again.

She tried for a few months. She sent me flowers, wrote me three letters that I tore up without reading. People told me she dedicated two columns "to a dear friend" who was obviously me, and I laughed: it sounded like the title of a Corín Tellado photonovel. Later, after the revolution, I learned Glória Veleno had joined a far-left party. I saw her a few times in the distance at protests, in clogs and long skirts, with carnations in her hair, chanting, "The people united will never be defeated." She supported the exoneration of those who had taught her everything about television and ended up gently distancing herself from those who, through the persistence of memory, might infect her with what she called "antibodies."

At the end of the 1970s, she started admitting to things. She gave interviews as a way to "openly admit to" her revolutionary past. Today, for example, she says on a TV news program, "I feel serene in admitting to my mature age." She got married, got divorced, remained friends with her former husband, her former bosses, even her former friends, albeit in their absence. She's an image consultant for a government minister, who praised the relevance of the criticisms she offered in her famous column Glória's World. She hosts a weekly interview program on television—*Glory with Glória*—and presumably has had plastic surgery on her nose and neck "because that's what scientific and technological progress is for: perfecting us. And perfection is my goal." She doesn't have children, but every Christmas she appears on magazine covers with chubby, sad-eyed orphans who are getting younger and younger every year, and thus complement her own revitalized youthfulness.

I've kept this photo of the old Glória, slim and radiant in the newspaper office where the two of us worked for so many years, because I don't want to live without grief. Natália doesn't understand how I can maintain a retrospective affection for someone who is ugly to her core. She chastises me: "You're just falling for the primitive subterfuge of external beauty." But that's not it. Beauty, wherever it comes from—inside or out—freezes life; it doesn't interest me. It appears too quickly, fully formed. I think that what I found so dazzling about Glória was the way that internal ugliness flickered dully in her external beauty, rounding it out, giving her a malign tinge of dark innocence. It is evil that leaves us bereft.

Ever since psychologists invented mourning, life has been taking place at a different speed, much faster, more action. I see more and more people solemnly heading to the movie theater whenever they get bowled over by their emotions, swallowing doses of Technicolor violence, hour after hour, until the pain crumples like a chewing gum wrapper forgotten in a pants pocket. Those who linger in their grief longer than the mental health guides recommend become cumbersome, as tedious as children—you never know what to say to them.

When Eduardo died I felt as if they'd opened up my chest and were sucking the blood from my heart, but people would tell me, "It's the kind of experience that makes you grow." When my best friend betrayed me, robbing me of the trusting nature I'd had since childhood, people would tell me, "It's the kind of experience that makes you grow." When I ended up out of work and out of friends and, deafened by the silence, reached out to somebody, the people on the other end of the line would tell me, "It's the kind of experience that makes you grow." Today I know I'm grown: I have no faith or joy or trust in anything in this world. It is only in the melancholy of these images, in which the pain always starts burning again as it did in the very first moment, that I feel my heart flush with blood and taste life's ravaged flavor.

7

São Pedro de Alcântara Overlook
Lisbon, April 25, 1974

Those aren't tears of happiness flooding Armanda's face as she sits on a garden bench with a red carnation pinned to her white knitted jacket. The women sitting on either side of her are strangers who stopped a moment to rest their legs after hurrying from Largo do Rato to Camões, and from there to Chiado, and then to Rossio, wanting to participate in every bit of the joy of the revolution at once. They were carrying bags full of milk, oranges, and carnations to pass out to the exhausted troops, and they were moved by the tears slicking Armanda's face. "My friend, the days of tears are behind us! Is your husband overseas, is that it? But listen, he'll be back really soon now that the people are the ones in charge! My son's in Angola, but on the radio they're already saying the war is over. Cheer up, honey!"

I had rushed out of the house at midmorning with my camera around my neck, holding Natália by the hand, with Jenny shouting after me, chasing me to the gate, saying I was crazy, irresponsible, trying to keep me from taking my little girl out into the dangers of the thronging city. I gave her a kiss, hugged her, promised to stay out of trouble, and raced to Baixa. On the crowded sidewalks, Natália and the other children played marbles and hopscotch between the adults' legs. People offered her bites of cake and pieces of chocolate. Sitting on the edge of the fountain in Rossio, we munched on sandwiches and apples. And in early afternoon, in Camões, I spotted Armanda running toward me with her arms spread wide, exhausted, sobbing. She'd been looking for me since morning—she'd called my house and combed the entire downtown area repeatedly. João Paulo, seemingly so solid, so ensconced in domesticity, so committed to his students, so thorough in tidying the house, had launched himself into outer space. He'd left her the night before. And, just like in a fado song, he'd traded her in for her best friend.

Everybody knew that the great love of João Paulo's life was actually São, and that he'd ended up marrying Armanda because she was the realistic replica of that unreal passion. Armanda and São had rented a room together back in college, and it was impossible to run into one of them without also seeing the other. And as João Paulo repeatedly and unsuccessfully attempted to catch São's eye, Armanda seemed to gradually transform into a carbon copy of São, but even more so. She walked, dressed, smiled, and smelled like her friend, her eyes always on João Paulo, who didn't even know she existed. After graduation, São got a job up in Porto, and six months later João Paulo married Armanda. Now, six years later, São had come back, and it seemed like this time João Paulo had gotten her attention. Armanda swore she'd been taken completely by surprise: before the previous night, she'd never suspected João Paulo of having the slightest interest in São, whose perfume she'd so diligently copied.

In its clear framing, this photo is proof that all images, even the most honest ones, can be a fraud. The tears from Armanda's eyes sparkle like a river that's overflowed its banks; the carnation, the women smilingly embracing her, the sun on their hair, the children—nothing betrays the trite drama that this moment on April 25 conceals.

Nevertheless, with the story of this photo revealed, it seems to me almost a premonitory symbol. In the years that followed, divorce would become a minor everyday tragedy. Reports from the period explained the avalanche of broken marriages as an unfortunate but natural consequence of freedom. After all, there seemed to be a multitude of couples bound together by duty, fear, habit, or resignation to whom the torrent of revolution, with its songs about the seagull that flew and flew, gave a liberating breath.

There may have been cases like that, with heroes out of a Camilo Castelo Branco novel who escaped being trapped in an unwanted marriage, but I never came across any. What happened to many people from my generation was infinitely more naïve and banal: they fell in love with politics, and they let the parties divide their hearts. The husband would align himself with communism, the wife with socialism or social democracy (which were still different things back then). Or the other way around. And they'd start yelling at each other. And so we witnessed a rise in the divorce rate among the country's educated elites. Ten years later, when it had become clear that democracy didn't guarantee peace, sustenance, health, and housing, and that earthly happiness still glowed in the faces of the same wealthy people as always, religion began to replace politics, and divorce expanded as a right of the masses. And so an army of women formed a separatist vanguard. Tired of working ever harder at home and in the factories, and in exchange for less security and less money, they sought rest in transcendence. Several of my companions left the home, entrusting their children to their doting husbands, and joined the guru Marahaji's spiritual communes that had sprung up on the peninsula south of the Tagus River.

Today, I read in Armanda's flooded eyes the hopelessness of that hope that has changed relationship dynamics for the better over the past twenty years. Yet the photo itself is divorced too: it fled from reality in search of intimacy. Today, nobody seems interested in witnessing anything—photojournalism has become an insignificant job, understood as a sort of ingenuous replication of reality. But there's no such thing as reality. That's what Armanda is telling me in the silence of this portrait of euphoria. Fashion photography and art photography, with their studied contrasts and their aesthetic staging carefully constructed down to the least detail—that is reality to me. I see those photos on the walls of galleries, so thoroughly products of their time, so sure of their allusive repertoire, and I turn away from them; aesthetic conventions still the vacillations of the gaze.

I've always preferred black and white. Color seemed too easily manipulated—and the world was black and white anyway. Now it is reality that appears to me in black and white, the reality of these days in which beauty has become obligatory and is governed by only a few rules: these accessories of absence are to contain completely smooth bodies and a sober symmetry of shadows. In the near future, we'll be able to select our faces from a catalog, and the faces of our dead idols will enter the public domain, as will the naïve notion of rebuilding success through a face. Maybe the vulgarization of beauty will end up rejuvenating the subjectivity that created art in the first place. The more intense a source of light, the less bearable it is to look at and the greater the shadow it casts, until only one side is visible. The twentieth century is an age of darkness. That's why it's so difficult to photograph, and that's why I work so hard. Jenny used to say my work was destroying me, but it's just the opposite: I work so as not to be destructive.

My work is something akin to love, and love, which we wished so urgently to democratize, eludes the best intentions. Love is a capitalist octopus; the more tightly it's squeezed by competition, the more it grows. When there's no more space for vertical expansion, it spreads horizontally, with variations in range and multiple by-products, over all the world's deformities—and what is ugliness, if not a truth that differs from the one we were coded for? That's why I'm so disgusted with the regime of beauty; that's why I'm more and more interested in shattered bodies. A critic once wrote about me, "This photographer isn't just good, she's malevolently good." My friends congratulated me. I felt profoundly alone. The critic thought, as is so common today, that my images resisting the canon of beauty were ironic, and that irony is proof of superior intelligence, and that intelligence is the illuminated side of evil. For me, those photos were just portraits of love. Like this one, of Armanda. Devastated and pregnant. Without even knowing it.

8

Jenny, Pedro, and António José
Chess House Garden, September 1976

The photos from the 1970s aged rapidly. The present loomed too large in the people and events, sprinkling an ashy layer of the ephemeral over the images. This portrait escaped that. It's as if my father, Uncle Tó Zé, and Mother Jenny were living tranquilly in another dimension. I found it while going through a box of photos after Jenny's death.

Her eyes commanded me, from inside the portrait, "Keep telling our story." It was a strange order; Jenny never told anyone to do anything. I started assembling scattered papers, notebooks that almost always broke off after the first few lines or pieces of photographic ephemera. And I gradually assembled this album from a handful of images. A whole life—or at least mine—can be summed up this way. Only afterward did I find out about Jenny's diary. In that notebook, she bade farewell to the clarity of life. As if she sensed the two years of agonizing dementia that still stood between her and the eternity of paradise. Jenny never doubted such a place existed. That's why she adjusted so well to the imitation of happiness.

The sky was dissolving into rain over the city that November morning when we found her dead on the living room floor, doubled over a plate of baby food that was swarming with flies. In recent years, Jenny had refused to eat solids, saying it was immoral to chew things in order to survive. The word *immoral* was one she'd never used in the past. In truth, she'd lost her teeth, her dazzling rows of immaculate teeth, and refused to replace them. "Dentures! You solve everything with prosthetics! In my day, people remained whole to the very end, and that's how I plan to die. Whole, intact," she'd say. Sometimes she'd add, with a philosophical air, "If God took my teeth, that means something. It means teeth are superfluous. I have to learn to eat soft things, easy things, like babies do."

The death of her husband had stripped her of any interest in being beautiful. She considered beauty a natural consequence of the act of loving and deeply despised all the conscious effort devoted to what she called "feminine ostentation." She mocked women who made themselves up "like those silly eighteenth-century duchesses, with their whore envy," and she thought plastic surgery, except in cases of serious accidents, was an affront to human greatness. She used to say art had become abstract as men and women became indistinguishable from each other, on a single assembly line of geometric beings, with identical faces and bodies. She'd see Michael Jackson on television, sigh, and say, "After centuries fighting for their racial dignity, blacks are now using household cleaners to try to look just like everybody else. Don't you dare say I'm old. Now that they've invented health to make people last longer, nobody wants to be old. And then they call me crazy." She was crazy, yes, but not so crazy that she ever forgot to take her blood pressure medication or her vitamins. She said she was determined to live out her old age to the end, defying an oppressively anti-wrinkle world and indulging in some robust cursing. She used to hear voices, held long conversations with the spirits of Uncle Tó Zé and my father.

But little by little those voices disappeared, and Jenny panicked. She stopped getting dressed in the mornings, ran through the house in her nightgown, shouting, disheveled. I once found her with her eyes wild and her arms, breasts, and genitals all scratched up. I moved into the house with her for a few months, and she calmed down. I managed to get her to start dressing and speaking normally, though she still clung to her diet of baby food and bananas mashed with orange juice.

By the end, she was nurturing fantasies of wild conspiracies with horticultural tenderness, as if tending flowerbeds planted with currents of air; she needed them to survive, to escape madness through power, to escape power through the harmony of opposites. At the end of the first month, I saw her out in the garden, furtively dumping the glass containing her dissolved medication into the fuchsias. That explained the flowers' perpetual vibrancy in contrast to her increasing pallor. I scolded her, and she bristled at me like a wildcat. She must have seen the idea of a psychiatric hospital flicker in my eyes, because a few minutes later she had softened as quickly as she'd lashed out. She offered a vague smile and started calling me sweetheart to convince me she was mentally sound. Though I wasn't convinced, I pretended everything was fine.

The truth is, I couldn't bear living in that house anymore, with that woman who was only the shadow of the Jenny who'd raised me. But I had to work up the courage to leave. She constantly railed against "executives" like me, calling us "maidservants urging on the poverty of the soul"; she sensed the hastening destruction of that world of sage uselessness that had been hers. I ended up returning to my own house, but I continued to visit her every day, or every other day, alternating with Natália.

It was almost as if she did it on purpose: she died while I was away. In October 1993 I went to Prague for five days to do some reporting. During those five days, in one of those coincidences that are as commonplace as they are improbable, Natália split up with her husband, Manuel Almada came down with the flu, and Jenny seized the opportunity to die, binding all of us together with the unshakable bond of guilt.

Natália was the one who gave me Jenny's secret diary: "Here, Mom. This belongs to you. It was written for you. But don't think ill of Grandma Jenny. She had a good life. And especially don't get annoyed with your father. He did the best he could." My daughter is always frightened by the excess of my judgments, just as I'm frightened by the excess of her forbearance. My fear is a stupid one: her generation's life is incompatible with the level of ethical stringency I'm used to. To tell the truth, that level of stringency always existed much more in our myths than in reality. But now that myth is falling apart in this age of fashionable Lycra. With the advent of democracy, it even stopped being possible (or, as they say, "feasible") to privilege being over any instance of having. All ambitions have their "context," and attitudes are removable decals, in bright or muted colors depending on the season. Everybody is responsible for personal and global issues alike—rainforests, individual success, hunger in Africa, depression, the construction of a unified Europe, pollution, emancipation of the masses, eternal youth—and so nobody feels the least responsibility for anything.

But when I read Jenny's diary I realized my father hadn't been the spineless playboy I'd sadly judged him to be. I'd spent my entire life keeping him delicately at a distance so as not to confront what I'd deemed his lack of love for me, and, before me, for my mother, and, before my mother, for any human being. His vehemence had seemed to me a salon affectation, and his extreme devotion to António a subservient cowardice. Dear Natália, Jenny's diary disturbed me enormously because it forced me to see, for the first time, beyond the comfortable protection of familiar set images, beyond rigid scientific descriptions of personality. Through her hand, your grandfather Pedro finally became my father. And I can judge only myself: for having failed to get beyond the visible letter of her words, to reach the mutely unanimous voice of those three hearts. Nevertheless, I find consolation in the lines of my portrait as Jenny paints it. I will strive not to flog myself too cruelly with posthumous recriminations, so as not to tarnish the minimal heroism of the daughter she so truly deserved.

Yes, at first I was annoyed with Jenny's secret, and her resignation to it. To tell the truth, I was annoyed above all with my own naïveté: to avoid seeing my father's romance with another man, I'd imagined Jenny as a stereophonic muse, the lover of both friends. That's why my initial response was to rebel against my father, against his enigmas and omissions. I felt sorry for Jenny, but in the end Jenny never lets anyone feel sorry for her. Her diary reveals, most of all, her implacability: when she'd decided that somebody was perfect, nothing could disabuse her of the notion.

9

Natália, Architecture Studio

July 1992

It's hard for me to look at this photo of my daughter as a woman. I have albums and albums full of her as a baby and as a little girl; when she was a teenager I started taking fewer photos of her, and more and more regularly I'd forget to organize them. Often, I didn't even get the film developed. It's normal for parents to pay more attention to their children's initial stages of growth. I still clearly remember her first smiles, and her early sentences, troublemaking, fears. At three years old, Natália hardly talked about anything else but "spookters," flesh-and-blood ghosts with all the awful powers of life. The word reflected the fascination and terror she felt for the various examples of the genre that appeared in the books she read. She would open a page, reluctantly look, and then start slowly backing away until, with a jump, she'd slam the book closed and burst into tears. Five minutes later she'd flee from social contact and reopen the book to another page, which would once more spark a tingle in her fingertips and at the backs of her eyes.

Now that all words seem to have been said already, attention to these early experiences is enormously useful for anyone with the bold aim of finding meaning, whatever it may be. Nonsense. The truth is, I don't like it that Natália's grown up. She's prettier than I am, smarter, and most of all happier. And insultingly young. That's what I don't like seeing.

When she was a little girl, I believed in maternal instinct. A young woman with a beautiful child in her arms naturally makes a certain impression. She doesn't have to say anything or have any special talents, because being a mother gives her a glowing aura that immediately sets her apart. I loved scandalizing the pious women who'd say to me, "What a pretty little girl! Is she adopted?" Smiling triumphantly, I'd reply, "No, no. I had her myself, with a fighter from the Mozambique Liberation Front." My father used to reproach me, claiming that such boasting only traumatized the child. "Oh," I'd retort, "so you've become a trauma spotter?" He'd shake his head, shrug, sigh, and not say anything else. My immense sense of righteousness only swelled.

Jenny used to say I was taking the family's sense of humor to a terrible extreme. According to Natália, I lack a sense of humor altogether: "It must not have been allowed in the fight for women's liberation. You all really did a terrific service, burning bras while holding children on your laps. You created a Virgin Mary who was even more studious than the old one, terrified of men and so very serious, she'd make the dead yawn. And all you did was get us saddled with even more work and scare off our prey." I know she refers to men as prey just to irritate me. And to make me jealous. But I pretend not to notice, explaining for the twentieth time that we never burned bras, only brooms, orange blossoms, and aprons, and that it was a purely symbolic act. She doesn't get it. She doesn't think it's funny. And I'm the one without a sense of humor.

It pains me that she doesn't even realize that it was those "extremist acts" by "strident women," as she calls them, that secured the rights that now seem so natural to her. She designs cities on this drawing board overlooking the Tagus. She read in some American books that women like her are called "postfeminists." A few days ago one of her friends said that "being a feminist has a historical connotation that is no longer appealing, and may even be a bit counterproductive." Natália laughed and said it was that discussion that wasn't appealing. But maybe she would have agreed with her friend if I hadn't been there.

I thought Jenny's illness and death would bring me closer to my daughter. Their complicity made me intensely jealous in a way that took me years to admit. Jealousy was one of the great taboos of my generation—Natália is right about that. But not even the moderation I've adopted in older age can facilitate a truce between us; Natália delights in pulling apart my contradictions, pitting my words against each other. I taught her to have more respect for herself than she did for any authority figure, and now I'm suffering the consequences of that broad-minded education. Jenny warned me. It seems I didn't manage to impart anything to them; nothing can expand my mother's or my daughter's consciousness. It's as if they never belonged to me. Natália, who lived inside me, alone inside me, for nine months, feeding off my love alone, still seems to belong to me less than Jenny does, who only inherited me.

More than a mother, I tried to be my daughter's best friend. But she never entrusted me with a single one of her tears. "You can't cry on the shoulder of a person who never cries," she told me. "But Jenny didn't cry either," I said. My daughter laughed and told me that all I was capable of weeping were tears of glass, like in photographs. I never would have lashed out at my mother that way, but Natália doesn't quite see me as a mother; I'm just an older woman trying to force out her secrets. And with Jenny's death, the gulf between us seems to yawn even wider.

I'd like to take pleasure in her success, but I can't. That's another function our children serve—consoling us for all that we never were. At least that's what we think when they're little; that's what I thought during the long nights I spent beside her cradle. I shuddered with fury and despair one morning when she appeared at breakfast looking gorgeous in my red dress. She'd intended it as homage, or to prove herself worthy of my admiration, but I see that only now. At the time, I perceived only that she was a beautiful nineteen-year-old woman and my clothing looked better on her than it did on me. "Do you like it?" she said, glowing with vanity. "No. I don't like you taking my things without asking," I replied. Startled, she was still able, as ever, to fire back: "Fine. I didn't realize you'd ended up embracing the notion of private property." Then she started preaching at me about how irresponsible I was. By then I'd dropped my regular work with newspapers and was scraping by as a freelance photographer. I wanted to control my time and choose my work, perfect my art, which meant my financial life wasn't exactly easy. Radiant in my red velvet dress, Natália harangued me about finding a job that provided retirement benefits, all the while stirring her coffee and chewing the scant half piece of toast she ate to avoid gaining weight.

A few months later I brought Álvaro home for dinner. Álvaro did public relations for a gallery where I'd had a show. He was thirteen years younger than I and seemed fascinated by my work. We kept running into each other with increasing regularity, and we'd spend hours lost in conversation. It seemed to me that by now it wasn't just work that brought us together. Natália decided to show up for dinner that evening wearing my white lace blouse and leather pants. Álvaro had eyes and words only for her. After he left I strictly forbade her from using my things. I never called Álvaro again, and he didn't call me either. Many years later, Jenny's diary confirmed my daughter's secret romance. I was surprised to see him show up at her wedding. Natália never talked to me about him, never brought him home. But I know it was her love for Álvaro that caused her divorce. Not that divorces really need a cause: like weddings, they are acts of peaceful rebellion.

I never regretted not having gotten married. I spared myself my friends' sad experiences, in which you can almost hear the fabric of human relationships slowly ripping over time. I became an expert in impossible men. And Natália is following in my footsteps, particularly since impossible men multiply in inverse proportion to the world's possibilities. We are both heirs to an absence that is beyond our control or understanding. Danielle's shadow, Xavier's shadow—they stand between us and the world, parching the atmosphere like a silent and endless sandstorm. I thought images could cure me, that I could patch the holes in my heart with the world's moments and stop the blood from gushing. I thought that love could be tamed and the dark side of maternal instinct made rational. I thought too much. Everything is written in the empty spaces that lie between one word and the next. The rest doesn't matter.

10

Self-Portrait

March 1994

I really like this woman who's serenely gazing out at me, camera in hand. She's me. I'm fifty-two years old. It's in the curvature of the fingers that the passage of time first becomes apparent. When I was studying photography the professor would prod the bones in my hands until he felt them pop, telling me my fingers were too stiff to accommodate the fluidity of the world: "Relax. Let go. Accept." To capture a moment's swift passage, we must do away with abruptness entirely. Let ourselves be carried away on the inner slowness of speed. As we age, our fingers grow emaciated and sinuous. Closer to time. Age spots flow over the skin of my hands, gradually spreading. When people mistreat me I stare at those brown islands that are leading me to the land of my dead. No one can do me harm anymore; a few more years, and maybe they won't even be able to leave a mark.

This is my only self-portrait. I decided to take it when I came home after the opening of my show on Mozambique. I'd had to wait thirty years to hang that show, thirty years till I could find the perfect space and the gentle atmosphere those images required. I also thought the heavy cloak of years would shield me from the carbon dioxide of visibility. But the people who came up to congratulate me said, "These photos are just fireworks with nothing to back them up." They said, "It's evident you weren't really at ease with the camera." They said, "As a document, they're interesting photos."

I asked my first photo editor to introduce the show. I thought he was the only one who could explain the power, the suffering, and the quality of those photos. He'd seen my beginnings from the inside, discussed angles and f-stops with me; when I called him Pygmalion he'd laugh and shake his head: "I was merely the humble discoverer of a great talent." Thirty years later, at my first major public show, my mentor didn't talk about talent. Well, strictly speaking, it was my talent he didn't mention. Instead he gave a long, animated speech about the genius of Werner Bischof, who'd photographed famine victims in India in the 1950s. In the last two lines of his speech, he referred to the "documentary vitality" of my photos, which would be inducted "into the same tradition of aesthetic and civic concerns as Bischof." And that was it. The attendees applauded the fire and erudition of his speech, and two minutes later they were whispering to each other, "He barely talked about Camila's photos. That says something."

After the show, I lay facedown across my bed, sobbing like a teenager, for more than an hour. I cried with rage that I was the only one who realized those photos of Mozambique were genuinely good. The best I'd ever taken. Much better than the portraits of shattered bodies that had earned me the erroneous descriptor of "malevolently good." Much better than all the aesthetic and antiaesthetic propaganda with which we shackle the circular decadence of light around each life. Much better—and, in fact, incomparable. Mine. I was fifty-two years old and I was alone. As alone as the day I was born, but much less lonely. I had a body, a job. A story, with its jubilant mantle of dead loved ones. So I decided to do this self-portrait, memorializing the moment when I truly started to like myself.

In my revolutionary youth, the verb *to like* was forbidden. It was understood that liking something indicated an inability to objectively, rationally, and intelligently analyze it. Liking was something insane minds did, minds that were confused about the structural categories of things, that took pleasure in an unsophisticated, emotional approach to problems. That insanity could be unconscious and involuntary—as was the case of the laborer and peasant classes, which were doomed to laziness of thought through the imposition of illiteracy—or conscious and intentional, as on the part of the dominant bourgeoisie, which refused to democratically accept progress in art. We never used to say that we liked or didn't like a movie, a book, a painting, or a person. We always tried to explain them and understand, keeping in mind their full context, the means used and the ends achieved. And declarations of love were replaced by confirmations of fact: "I feel really good when I'm with you"; "We make a good team." Love was just further unhappy proof of the world's injustice, a fate that would befall only poorly exercised minds. Though I succumbed to the weakness of romantic love, I never committed the mortal sin of loving myself. I had erected good defenses. When those ideological defenses began to crumble, I used my camera to remain impregnable. Now I needed to turn that camera on myself.

I like this woman with gray eyes ringed by purple hollows. I like this woman's scanty eyebrows, the wrinkles that reduce the color of her eyes to a flash of light. I like her gaunt cheeks, her sharp jawline, the way you can practically see her bones through her skin. I like her smooth mouth, without color or volume. I like the folds on her neck, like a map that's become crumpled after many journeys. This woman printed herself whole on her life and knows that she's going to die. Nobody can do her any harm anymore, nobody can even leave a mark on her near-weightless body.

Natália's Letters

"I don't know how to pretend I love very little when everything inside me thrums with love."

—*Vergílio Ferreira*

1

Lisbon, May 21, 1984

Dear Jenny,

Right now I'm crying in my room, all alone. I turn
the music up loud to keep you from realizing that I've
inherited more than just your incredible gift of joy
that sets the world ablaze wherever we go.

Of course, you know that gift comes at a price, and
I know you'd pay double if you could—you'd suffer in
my place the loneliness and melancholy that plague eter-
nity-seekers like us. But you can't—your warm lap is no
longer enough to protect me from the world. And so I'm
hiding these tears from you because they'd make you sad.

Maybe I won't even send this letter—you don't
deal well with grand declarations of love.

I discovered early on, from my mother's photographs, that happiness is a collection of moments,
suspended outside of time, that are revealed only after
they've become yellowed by absence. In those photos
I learned not to fear love or longing, and I, too, in
my own way, without her even noticing, became a

capturer of light. In the precise movement of her long fingers on those instruments she used to flee from life, I discovered eroticism as the premonition of a wound, an endless task of remembrance. I carry in my blood that is also hers a quiet passion for lost loves, a determination to understand the essence of things only afterward, to love distance as the only way to be close to heaven. I fell wildly in love, began to fill my childhood room with smoke and tears; that's why I feel so close to it, to that static adolescence like a meek and brutal illness, an incurable blood wound that feeds off a sepia-toned music we euphemistically call pain.

I know you experienced love as a vast infatuation with the world and with other people. I remember clear as day what you said when I, at thirteen, had a crush on a boy whose indifference made me weep tears of rage: "Sweetheart, love is never a dependence. It's an abundance, and we continue to experience love out of need. We encumber love with everything we can't find a place for." Yes, I know: we saddle it with loneliness, personal affirmation. My mother rails daily against women who need a man to feel good about themselves. And just think of the irony, Jenny: I stole the man she so urgently needed to feel good about herself. It wasn't out of spite. It wasn't on purpose. But that doesn't lessen my crime.

At first, I confess, I was driven by a certain wickedness, which today I'd prefer to call naughtiness. When Álvaro came to the house for dinner, I decided to play the femme fatale to show my mother I wasn't a little girl anymore. And to punish her for trying to seduce a man who was far too young for her. You can call me prejudiced, Jenny, but experience suggests that in these situations age always works against women. Álvaro would only have made her suffer. Go ahead and laugh: my mischief turned around on me, and Álvaro made me suffer instead. Just like that. She doesn't even need to know.

But I do take comfort in the idea that I was able to seduce a man who was interested in my mother. I do criticize her a lot, and it's true I'm irritated by pretty much everything about her. But most of all I'm terrified that I'll never come close to measuring up. Camila withstood prison and torture, while the mere thought of giving blood makes me shudder. Camila can eat whatever she wants without getting fat, and I can't stand the patronizing affection with which she tells me I'm lucky to be half black because I'll never be cursed with cellulite. Which is a lie anyway. Camila has an artistic gift, and I'm afraid I may lack the obsessive quality necessary to discover even a potential flicker of talent. It was despair that drove my mother to photography. I once defiantly declared that photography is just a collection of dead people. A morbid art. She laughed: "That's why I like it." Today, it seems to me that even despair is difficult. Or at least it's difficult to pursue it to the very end.

I never thought I could really like a man who wore a ponytail and rustic Alentejo-style boots. When he showed up at the gallery a week after that dinner, I had just one objective: to seduce him and then immediately cast him aside. I wanted to crush my mother's newfound youthful enthusiasm—she'd recently started going to the gym in the mornings and trying on dresses in the mirror. She'd even gone so far as to express interest in having another child and was sighing longingly at babies. So I went out to dinner with Álvaro.

Afterward, we went for drinks at Frágil, where I ran into my friend Leonor with some of our friends from university. They were celebrating Nuno's upcoming show, which had just been arranged right there, ten minutes before our arrival, for two weeks later. Nuno claims that if you want to build a career, you have to be in the right place at the right time. The right time will be sometime between one and six in the morning, either at Frágil or Noites Longas. In the past, when we were pulling an all-nighter at somebody's house to finish a group project, Nuno would leave at midnight, having put gel in his hair and straightened his tie, saying, "Keep going without me, if you don't mind. I have to go to work." His work, as became clear that night, is at Frágil. For months he'd been floating among the drinks and lights with two or three sketches under his arm in a discreet folder and a well-orchestrated plan of attack. That night, the owner of an excellent gallery of new work was complaining about a date conflict that was hampering her upcoming presentation of a new genius of Spanish painting. Nuno pounced immediately with his project *Virile Age*. The gallery owner liked the concept, an installation in which found objects would be exhibited side by side with paintings, collages, and sound recordings, using a juxtaposition of registers to ironically deconstruct the myths and modes of masculinity. They set the opening for two weeks later.

Nuno was no coward, but he was clearly terrified, as evidenced by the way he kept fidgeting with his tie. The problem, it seemed, was that his entire oeuvre consisted of those sketches. Smoking furiously, the artist mused, "My approach employs not a single style, but several. Postmodernism isn't a rebel; its forebears were, but it doesn't have that luxury—its career is on the line." Clara was clearly dazzled, so Graça went on the counterattack, arguing that as a matter of fact our generation's greatest artists are profoundly subversive, incorporating obsolescence into their works as a way of condemning the alienating speed of the present moment. Leonor, who was listening to this erotic repartee with great interest, mentioned an amazing book by Paul Virilio that discussed precisely this issue. But Nuno wasn't listening anymore. He let his eyes drift over the dancing girls and announced, in a smothered voice, that he had to get some air, look for inspiration. So we trailed after him to Noites Longas.

Álvaro wasn't much of a talker. Actually, I think that's the secret of his success with women. He has a marvelous ability to seem to be paying attention. He rests his eyes on the victim and punctuates her sentences with a rhythmically repeated "Mm-hmm." Without realizing it, I'd told him my entire life story and still didn't know a thing about him. As we went out into the courtyard at Noites Longas, a tall blonde draped herself around his neck and kissed him on the mouth. Álvaro laughed, tousled her hair, and kept walking. I pulled him inside to the dance floor, where a mournful tango floated in the air, and danced with him till dawn. When we left, pursuing the aroma of freshly baked bread, I no longer wanted to cast him aside. And it's been hell ever since, Jenny.

Maybe Álvaro belonged to my mother's generation after all, which frowned on "grand emotions." They were afraid of losing their heads and succumbing to the foolish whims of the devil of Stupidity. Or that the inflexible god of Reason and Justice might punish them for indifference to the class struggle. They fled from any path to happiness that evoked fearsome echoes of respectability.

He makes love to me as if my body might offer him salvation. He gives himself to me and then slips through my fingers like sand. He sends me flowers one day and then tells me he's not looking for commitment the next. He mocks my dreams, says there's nothing left to architect and that I'd be better off going into interior design or fashion, or at least the textile industry. He's accustomed to thinking everything is relative and it's impossible to judge anything.

Sometimes I think: maybe he, too, is a product of this regime of indifference and regurgitation that we call the postmodern era, which seems utterly compatible with Portugal's longstanding apathy. Sometimes I think love is actually alienating to him because, up close, he finds human nature repellent. Excuses, you'll say, Jenny. A twisted way of thinking, cringeworthy, I know. At the very least, it's clear my lover will never win the Great Human Depth Award. I'd deserve better, were love something a person could deserve.

You can't imagine what a relief it's been to write you this letter, Jenny. It's lifted my spirits. In the end, this story could have been a much more tragic one: after all, Álvaro was almost the father of a sibling that I prevented from being born.

A kiss from your
Natália

2

Quinta de São Gabriel, January 5, 1990

Dear Jenny,

How does a person keep her friendships polished and gleaming for an entire lifetime? I believed the intimate time scale on which they are measured would always outstrip real time—especially since, strictly speaking, real time no longer exists. Only an abrupt absence. Sometimes I worry I'll reach thirty without once having seen my own image reflected in the swift-flowing river of my twenties.

But there doesn't seem to be an alternative: if I stop running, I'll never be free. I have to work hard, prove my worth, or nobody will take me seriously. As soon as you get to college, you realize life isn't going to go easy on anyone who doesn't give it her all. I know things weren't like that in your day. Or even my mother's. But try to understand. University studies may be intense, but they're nothing compared to what's waiting for us on the other side. Back at the beginning of the 1980s, which ended only five days ago, we had time to spend endless nights in conversation. Now we're all grinding away thinking we'll have time again when we're thirty-five.

It's not money or even success that's driving us, believe me. Fine—it's not just that, at least. I chose architecture because I thought it was the only art form where the idea of social responsibility could still survive without being mocked. Where the great imperative of freedom could still be exercised with an altruistic aim, transcending the frivolous combinatory fantasy that holds sway in this time of constant personal reinvention. But architecture also kneels before the god of ostentation. In keeping with the era, this god is garbed in the robes of hardship. But it is an expensive hardship, omnipotent, without an exterior. The avant-garde has nestled into the system and now quickly co-opts any herald of alternative action. In fact, money has gradually come to dominate everything: without it you can't get a place to live, let alone the books, movies, and travels we need in order to change the world. That's revolution these days. It's sad, but there's no other option.

You're going to tell me my generation lacks the generosity that, back in your day, expanded the houses' walls and transformed a crust of bread into a feast. It's true. I think the time of miracles has come to an end. Manna doesn't fall from the heavens, or at least it's no longer free. You taught me that adversity always masks any sign of happiness, and I wonder whether this scarcity of resources might be the result of the otherwise desirable phenomenon of extended life expectancy. We last longer on the earth, and that allows for lives that enrich our hearts but consume our spoils. It's also possible that houses have started aging differently: they are shrinking, becoming tiny and unattainable. There are no tumbledown fixer-uppers available, only luxurious rehabs.

That's why I was so excited to get a call from Leonor inviting me to a birthday party "like we used to have" on her family's farm in the Douro Valley. Leonor's birthday is January 4, and she used to throw a huge party, usually with a theme and everybody in costumes. This time she decided to bring our college friends back together. Only the core group, and no costumes. And here we are. Me and Leonor, Graça, Quicas, Clara, Nuno and his wife, Ângela and her husband. At first I wrinkled my nose at these unfamiliar hangers-on—what was supposed to be a reunion of good pals had become a coming-out party for newlywed couples. I whispered to Leonor that if I'd realized how things were going to be, I'd have brought Rui. "Don't be stupid," she told me. "Rita and Fred are already part of the group. They're great, you'll see. You don't know them, that's all."

The weather seemed to be going all out for our reunion. A cloudless sky, the pale, nearly white blue of childhood casting a golden light over the brown earth. We went to Régua for lunch, real sausages and black pudding and corn-and-rye bread, all washed down with a red wine that awoke our memories. We dredged up fun times that had long since been forgotten. We took photos in the ridiculous poses we'd used as students. We returned home at dawn. I suggested we hold out another hour so we could watch the sunrise over the mountains, but nobody seemed to have the energy for it. "We're just old, I guess," I teased. But it's not that. We'd played cards the whole night. And after a while, we started playing for money. Don't worry, Jenny, dear, I'm not going to adopt my grandfathers' vice: greed was merely a pretext for excitement, as it seems we can no longer play simply to win or lose, to exchange barbs and laugh uproariously the way we used to. By the time we'd polished off a turkey, a cheese plate, and a few spoonfuls of pudding, we'd gotten everybody up to speed. Each of us had provided some general information about our current activities, and conversation started to flag. We did a little reminiscing, cautiously ribbed each other.

These days, nobody really knows who gets along with whom. I suggested we play a game of Scruples for old times' sake. They shook their heads: "Scruples, at this hour? What a drag." And ethereal Graça, bewildered Graça, who so often used me as a confessional vault for her secret love triangles, added jokingly, "It's dangerous playing those games with you. You can find out our secrets. I'd be in real trouble if you knew my secrets!" As she spoke, she was parting my hair into two braids, just like she used to. That's how she honored her childhood dream of being a hairdresser. Afterward, she gave me a quick hug and a loud kiss, like the old days. Everything about Graça is loud: the gesticulations of her plump arms; her mousy hair that she started dyeing purple when she was sixteen; her small teeth, pale as grains of rice.

As the night wore on, the silences became denser and heavier. I recalled those Saturday afternoons we used to spend at Quicas's house. The door was always ajar, and music—invariably blues—would be rising from the bottom of the stairs. Everybody would bring something to drink or a packet of cookies. We'd arrive, claim a cushion or a spot on the sofa, grab some books and magazines—Quicas would wear the same black jeans and gray T-shirt for weeks at a time, but he had a huge collection of art and comic books—and stay there, silently reading and listening to music, for hours. And the silence then was a warm liquid that enveloped us.

Now Quicas had sprinkled talcum powder on a grease stain that had marred his Ralph Lauren shirt, and we desperately needed the company of words. Things were getting uncomfortable. "Did you get any nice gifts this Christmas?" Leonor asked, playing the good hostess. Nuno, Graça, and Fred, whose name is Alfredo, started listing theirs: "I got a beautiful anthology of Portuguese poetry, leather-bound and nicely illustrated, with a card from the secretary of culture," Nuno said. "Oh, you should see the set of Vista Alegre teacups I got! With a really nice card from the president of the Architecture Board that he signed himself," Graça said. "You've arrived, babe. A total success," said Fred, lighting a cigar. "Cuban cigars. Super expensive. Help yourselves. We've got to celebrate Leonor's aging." Leonor thought back and described a gorgeous paperweight, designed in Italy, that she'd been given by a Spanish bank whose headquarters she had remodeled. Clara shrugged and yawned. There was a little quibbling between Nuno and his girlfriend, Rita, who hissed at him loud enough for all of us to hear, "The card from the secretary of culture was for me. Yours was from the press secretary."

I don't know these people, Grandma. Four years ago, I loved all their joys and sorrows with all my heart. I lied many times for every one of them. I frantically telephoned Leonor's boyfriend's house on hundreds of occasions: "Call your mother! I told her you'd gone to the café, but I think she's wondering why you're spending the weekend at my house if you're just going there for hours on end." I took almost all of Graça's math exams for her.

I dropped a well-paid project because they'd cheated Nuno. But I was no hero. All of them did similar things for me. Even Clara, who, with her round glasses perched on the tip of her sharp nose, preached selfishness as her core guiding principle, did two all-nighters with me back in school to help me finish the barracks reconversion project that secured me a spot at the architecture studio where I still work today. That's the way the world was.

I really miss you, Jenny. I feel your absence keenly. I don't even know if I'll be brave enough to stick this letter in the mail. I'm just writing to assuage this sudden yearning. I spent half my life chiding you for reconstructing people according to your own design, and now I want you to teach me the magic formula—I need to know what to do so I can believe that these people are something that we know, deep, deep down (because, sadly, we're not just kindhearted but also very intelligent people), they are not. However hard I try, I remain in a state of pure myth: faith or despair. I don't know how to pretend to see what I do not see. I wanted to be like Grandpa Pedro, who accepted people's multitude of imperfections with all the naturalness in the world: to him, disappointment was a given, so it didn't even hurt. But how could he stand living like that? No, actually, I wanted to be like Jenny, so I filled people with the color of my dreams and deliberately ignored everything that wasn't part of my plan. But how does one pull that off?

Where can I find that pure happiness I used to feel on Christmas Eve? I'd already discovered that real life featured a lot of bad men—despite all appearances, I'm no dummy, and you and my mother provided me with an excellent education. Even so, naïvely, I thought I could maintain my own small world full of special people and almost special people, and create a complete life from there. Why do people fail so much in such trivial things? Leonor, for example. Yesterday we went out for a stroll through the vineyards, humming as we tramped down the hill toward the river, and all she talked about was her resentment of other people's happiness. She clearly spends her life worrying about how people see her. The girl who always used to speak her mind will now do whatever it takes to please God and the devil. I don't believe in either. And then she's surprised the world doesn't applaud her in accordance with her studied sociability. She no longer snatches the crispiest turkey drumstick for herself. She no longer lounges around with a book after meals, saying, "Let the men clear the table. I'm tired— I'm a member of the weaker sex, after all." She doesn't even hiss at me in a dire voice, "Careful, sweetie, you don't want to get fat. You know what's worse than a black woman? A fat black woman." I used to grab her arm and say, imitating the cadence of a slave's speech, "If white mistress need black woman to lend her boyfriend, black woman can offer couple of paler fellows. That no problem." Now Leonor greeted me with a big hug and said, "Darling! You just get prettier and prettier. It's like you don't age."

The sun of the fifth day of the 1990s has been shining on the Douro River for almost an hour. The water is a sheet of dark silver, moving very slowly. As if that opaque silver concealed not life, but some mechanical apparatus. I watched the sunrise by myself from the window in this cold, empty room, its damp walls hung with faded portraits of century-old ghosts. I don't know what I'm doing here.

A very sad kiss from your
Natália

3

Lisbon, May 6, 1990

Dear Jenny,

Sometimes it's not easy to talk to you. Ever since Grandpa Tó Zé died and Grandpa Pedro followed soon after, you seem really distant. I never imagined you needed them so much—you always struck me as an independent woman, more focused on the small rotations of your own little world than on other people's presence in it. Probably I made that up about you, and now that I no longer recognize you, I'm writing to you in an attempt to maintain that fiction. I confess I was startled today when I saw you. I'd never noticed before how much you'd aged; I'd ignored your crumpled body, your veins protruding like bones, your translucent hair. It was as if time had been carefully hidden beneath your crystalline dresses, prevented from expanding past the silver bun that shone like a beacon on the back of your neck.

Instead of my Jenny, today I encountered a sort of white witch garbed in a nightgown and with

disheveled hair, a wild look in her eyes, cackling madly. All my life I've run away from my mother to be
with you. Today I wanted to run away from you, and
it was my mother who reassured me. "Wait," she said.
"Think of her as being in a trance—this isn't Jenny. We
have to help her come back to us." Then my mother
started shooting furiously, pointing her camera and
telling you to smile, binding you up in stories, telling you António was coming soon and you needed to
be pretty and happy for him. "Happy," you repeated,
somewhat calmer now, "yes, I'm the happiest woman
in the world." It still seemed like you were in a trance.
Maybe you were just pretending to be calm so we'd
leave you alone. In any case, my mother managed to
pull a knitted dress over your head. You insisted you
were expecting visitors and ordered us out.

Visitors, poor thing. The stream of visitors has gradually slowed to a trickle as commitments and celebrity
draw them to other places. The person who's complaining about having too many visitors now—and with
good reason—is Manuel Almada, if you can believe it.
After a lifetime of aristocratic penury, he was named
president of the Foundation for the Development of
the Arts. Now he's constantly flooded with invitations
and gifts, beloved in all quarters of the country's upper
crust. He endures it stoically, eluding a dozen lunches
and dinners a day and remaining true to his old habits. That's why I'm so fond of him. Sometimes we fall
out of contact for months. I was a little worried when
he was chosen because I was afraid he'd think of me
as just another hanger-on. He called me up, sound-
ing hurt: "You forgot about your old beau, is that it?"

He's my most powerful friend, in every sense of the word. And of the ones who have, as they say nowadays, gotten ahead in life, he's the only one who can't stand talking to his close friends via secretaries, who are now called assistants. Indeed, nothing irritates him more than that particular aspect of nouveau-richeness. "But it does make it a lot easier to decide how to distribute the grant money, my dear," he explains with that Cheshire Cat grin of his. "When I get a phone call from a secretary telling me that Mr. So-and-So would like to speak to me, I cross him off my list. It's essential to have some kind of criteria, and since there's no way to objectively evaluate projects' quality at this point, because everything depends on context, I apply this decontextualizing criterion. It saves me a tremendous amount of work. There aren't many candidates left by the end." Dearest Jenny, Manuel Almada is your only visitor these days. I hope you at least see that Manuel is worth more than all your old relationships put together, which are like pollen blown to other parlors by the winds of the passing years.

But what I wanted to tell you is that I found your old friend Delfim Veleno. First, I need to tell you that you were wrong about him. Do you remember that long-ago day when Veleno declared, in an unusual fit of humility, "I don't think I'm cut out to be a novelist"? Well, I don't remember it either, but my mother loved to tell that story when she was trying to get you to laugh. According to her, you'd quickly and firmly agreed: "I don't think so either. You're incapable of impregnating your own soul, let alone other people's." I think the statement stuck with my mother because of the pregnancy metaphor, which to be honest, between you and me, didn't even seem like it was yours. But anyway. At that, Veleno's modest supply of modesty ran out and he stormed off, slamming the door behind him. And now it turns out that his is the redemptive quill that will transform Portuguese literature forever. And my friend Sebastião Lucas is the one who discovered him.

I believe I've already told you about Sebastião Lucas, who runs a publishing house, Penélope. It's fairly small—or as small as is really possible with a successful venture. The secret of Sebastião's success—which has been recognized by the President of the Republic himself, who gave him an award last June—is that he prudently alternates the avant-garde works with sumptuous coffee table books. All of the volumes are visually sober and elegant. The coffee table books are wildly expensive but sell like hotcakes, and it's easy to find organizations willing to subsidize them.

Sebastião has invited me to do a book about the tiles of Lisbon, with funding from both the city council and a tile factory. I was with him yesterday, working out some of the details, and at the end of our meeting he invited me to accompany him to the Júlio de Matos psychiatric hospital, where he was going to scout for new writers. Don't laugh, Grandma. In your day, insanity could probably go hand in hand with what we call normality. And there weren't so many publishing houses back then either. Sebastião says that people who can't adapt to our fast-paced civilization get put in hospitals, and that's where you have to go to find the truly creative souls.

He's a tough man, Sebastião is—he's not swayed by appearances. Just yesterday I saw him reject out of hand a book of short stories pitched by a tall, slender girl, very poised, pretty face, little pearl necklace, and an embroidered blouse. He didn't even glance at the title. He just shook his head forthrightly: "I don't have time at the moment, and besides, we're not taking on new authors." He told me he gets visits from about twenty young men and women a day, people he's never met before, says you can tell from a mile off they're spoiled brats convinced of their own genius. "What I'm interested in is difference—voices from the margins, poetry by rebels, drunkards, outcasts, people who can't get anyone to listen to them and have truly experienced the abyss, you know?"

The way time passes in that hospital reminds me of an aquarium. The distance between the sane and the insane dissolves in the denseness of the groves of trees that blot out the chaotic tumult of life outside the hospital. We sit down in a colorless room, almost empty of furniture, and one after another a nurse brings in the patients who write. They have shaky hands, dirty nails, tobacco-stained fingers, crumpled and ragged stacks of paper, sometimes almost illegible. Sebastião patiently assesses each page. We were heading toward the exit, disheartened, when we were intercepted by a stout, balding man in a shabby dark-red blazer and too-short pants that must once have been white. Though he was panting, he kept hopping up and down in excitement as he pleaded with an exceedingly courteous Sebastião to stay just a moment longer and take a look at his work.

I never would have recognized him, Jenny. I remember him as being redheaded with a neatly trimmed mustache and an elegant, impersonal voice—the voice of a man whose speech was built on the art of imitation. I knew him primarily as Glória's father, of whose cowardice the daughter presented a flawless reproduction. He was my mother's admitted betrayer, a lickspittle, a soul hollowed out by conformism, shaped by the prevailing aesthetic and ethical values of the powers that be. As Sebastião read his manuscript, Delfim stared at me intently and his eyes brimmed with tears. "Camila!" he said. "How you've changed! Your skin's so dark now! What happened?" Then he asked after you, Jenny, and started crying harder. I tried to explain that I wasn't my mother, but he wasn't listening. He apologized for not having been able to get me out of prison and asked me if I'd ever made up with Glória. He said Glória really liked me, that she had a good heart. He whispered in my ear that she always comes to see him late at night when she gets off work, tiptoeing past the nurses so they don't catch her, and tucks him in.

I later learned that Delfim had gone mad in the home where his daughter placed him after her mother's death. She never visited. Glória's intuition betrayed her, dear Jenny. In her effort not to think about her father, she ended up setting him on the path toward the pantheon of literature. Sebastião says Veleno is the Portuguese Genet, and that his novel, viscerally titled *Throw Me to the Wolves*, is going to be a huge bestseller.

I hope this news might help you return to our world, my dearest, dearest Jenny.

Many kisses from your
Natália

4

Lisbon, November 14, 1990

Dear Jenny,

"It's weird, you never talk about Rui," Leonor said to me a few days ago. I said that's why people get married: so they can talk about other things. But I remembered that's what you used to say too. So I started listing Rui's good qualities: the solidity of his presence, the sturdiness of his soul, the depth of his gaze, the contours of his body. My friend listened intently and said, "Sweetie, you just described a building!" Just as well. That's my life's work, after all: constructing buildings. Maybe it helps make up for my own missing foundation. One day I'll go to Mozambique in search of my father's memory.

Leonor always says, maybe to comfort me, that sometimes you're better off not having a father. After all, her father abandoned her by the side of the road when she was seven years old, holding her five-year-old brother by the hand, just because the boy had suddenly gotten sick and vomited on the leather seats of the father's brand-new Porsche convertible. She says she still remembers it like it was yesterday, the terror she felt as she walked along the road, trying to soothe her inconsolable baby brother until, sometime after nightfall, she came upon a bar with a telephone and was able to call her mother. Her father lost the right to unsupervised visits, which suited Leonor just fine. She says that incident is one of her only childhood memories: "Events, dreams, fears, elementary school, nothing. I don't remember *me*. Weird, right?"

There's nothing the least bit weird about Leonor; she embodies method, order, harmony, and pragmatism. Which, when you think about it, actually makes her pretty weird. Her house doesn't go with that subdued image either. She transformed every piece of furniture into a unique canvas: bed, coffee tables, chairs, desk—she painted them all so nothing matched. The chairs became a baroque concoction of gold stars, anchors, and stylized blue angels, while the bed was subjected to thick layers of abstract reds and ochres. I don't know how she can sleep in the middle of that chaos. She switched out the stove that came with the house for a secondhand one from the fifties, which she immediately painted hot pink. The house's contents are profoundly dissonant with its style.

It's one of those Portuguese buildings from the early seventies, with service stairs leading up to a rear door that opens right into the kitchen, next to which is the maid's bedroom with its tiny bathroom. Those houses may be sunny, but they're as gloomy as orphans, created for a short-lived civilization of bourgeois comfort—you really feel the absence of the servants, who somehow haunt them whenever you accidentally ring one of the now useless bells found on the walls of each room. When I mentioned those ghostly objects to Leonor—who had clearly never noticed them before—she let out a thin laugh: "That explains why my maid's been so lackadaisical. Back at my mother's house she was prompt and willing. Ever since she came to work with me here, she shows up late and just drinks tea, and if I ask her to stay on an extra half hour, she threatens me with the law. Those servant ghosts must be messing with her."

As 1985 began, coinciding romantic disappointments drove the two of us to flee to a beach in Alentejo. Sometimes I miss being as unhappy as I was on those glorious days we spent together. It couldn't have been better: Leonor, impeccably organized as always, had managed to get out of all her work and social obligations and arrived the night before at the little seaside cabin we'd rented.

I'd promised to get there by late afternoon, but I didn't manage to leave Lisbon until nightfall, a newly minted driver temporarily responsible for my mother's practically brand-new Fiat Panda. In my excitement I spaced out and got lost taking an unlit shortcut, and ended up crashing the car into a pile of rocks in the middle of a moonless night. And so I showed up at our rented house at the stroke of midnight astride a moped driven by an ancient Rambo of the fields—and she thought it was funny. I think she was even surprised at my self-assured manner—and I liked that, because I myself was terrified at my own daring. Any other person would have shot me an accusing, self-righteous look: "How could you be such an idiot? Don't you know how to drive?" Instead, it seemed to me, she admired me. As did, to be honest, my moped Stallone: "What are you doing out here at night all by yourself? Don't you have a husband or, say, a boyfriend?" the man had asked, in pajamas, lowering his shotgun. No, I didn't.

I'd walked for a while in the pitch black, unable to see a thing, until I spotted the light of that little house. I tried to head toward it, but I was stopped short by barking dogs, so I started shouting for help. That was when the man showed up, wearing long johns like the kind you see in cartoons, with a flap that snapped shut in the back, and holding a shotgun: "What's going on out here to make a woman carry on like that?" He was relieved to find he wasn't going to have to deal with a rapist while still half-asleep. I waited in the kitchen while he drew back the curtain that separated it from the bed, where his wife was rubbing her eyes. Then he took me back to the car on his moped, told me the steering column was definitely damaged, and warned me not to leave any suitcases in the car, since the coast was awash in thieves and smugglers: "You'll be lucky if the car's still got tires when you come back tomorrow." Under his breath, he muttered, "What makes women think it's a good idea to go out wandering around by themselves in the middle of the night?"

During those hours, I discovered there is nothing irredeemably dire about the world. When the car came to that abrupt halt and I found myself lost in a starless void, with the sea roaring menacingly somewhere in the distance, I crossed a boundary beyond which all fear was shattered. And Leonor sensed it immediately.

She could always read me like a book—a notion that seems trite only because it's exceedingly rare. After graduation, our lives went in different directions. We met up again six months ago for a joint work project and found that our friendship remained unaltered.

Unlike my mother, I've always been more interested in buried connections than in the spectacle of rupture. It's a way of maintaining my faith in a kind of happiness, dear Jenny, perhaps the only way of maintaining consistency without seeming ridiculous or weak. My era, after all, is one marked by dynamism and the relentless pursuit of pleasure. It's the philosophy of a generation that's doomed to hanging, and it makes me shudder. So much so, in fact, that I got married because of it. I relish Rui's absence—I think I already told you he's up in Coimbra, that's the only place he was able to get a spot in his specialty, and he comes home on the weekends. It seems like when he's not here his movements undulate through the house with a twinkling that his natural, and perhaps excessive, enthusiasm tends to stifle.

Rui is ardor in action. At first I didn't know if I should get annoyed or make a break for it. I ended up asking him to marry me one day as we were leaving the movie theater, suddenly bothered by the idea of returning to the sterile silence of my room. I was getting frustrated with how life lacked the compact humanity of the nineteenth-century novels I read almost addictively, and that radiant wholeness sped like an ambulance through the dark gleam of his eyes. Álvaro, like everybody else, was made up of loose pieces, a perpetually incomplete LEGO set, encompassing infinite and ever-changing possibilities. Rui, on the other hand, is what in the past would have been called a character. You always know what he's thinking, even on the rare occasions when he forgets to tell you. And he's always thinking about everything. He's just as interested in the Middle East crisis as he is in Madonna's latest album, in vitro fertilization, the controversy over Heidegger, or Manoel de Oliveira's next film.

I try to maintain a similarly dizzying array of contacts and stimulation to keep from missing him. Plus, he demands it: up in Coimbra he doesn't have friends, art openings, movies. He calls me every day. He never writes: he says he doesn't have time, and I don't actually feel like writing to him either. It's been a long time since I've been with Leonor just the two of us, letting the hours pass unheeded, talking about intimate, frivolous things over a bottle of old port and a loaf of homemade bread. Rui is always hanging around with a vivacious herd of young doctors who are just as impassioned as he is about the multimedia spectacle of human existence.

All Leonor and I need is just the barest hint of an expression. During those first days of the new year that we spent in each other's confidence, I remember sitting with her on the seashore, sucking on tangerines and inventing stories about passersby, howling with laughter at the way we finished each other's sentences with uncanny instinct. I remember the sun dissolving into infinite twinkles in her green eyes. I remember telling her I wanted to have a baby with Álvaro, and how she replied, with a freckled smile tinged with malice, "What for? So you can give your mother the little sibling she wanted to give you?"

Oh, Jenny, you can't imagine how grateful I am that you never asked me, "So when are you going to have a baby?" Even my mother did that. Well, maybe in her case, given the circumstances, it's not so strange. But Rui's family too. Last weekend we went to visit his parents, and I left there wanting to remain an aunt forever, which seems to be the modern version of the old-school bra burner, at least in that pious family. Christ! They spent the evening asking me when it was going to be my turn, and wasn't it embarrassing to have been left behind by my sister-in-law, who's younger than me and already pregnant? At first I replied politely that I wasn't in a rush or jealous; then, in a brusquer tone, I said it wasn't a race; and finally, viciously, that I like the life I've got just fine and would rather spend my mornings lounging in bed with a man. At that, my sainted husband broke in diplomatically, explaining to those present that we have very busy lives and that just a little while back we were living in a dump.

His grandmother, a sort of Miss Marple without the mystery, shook her head determinedly and said that didn't mean anything, plenty of people live in a dump and have ten or twelve children, and even raise them better than people of means do. When I suggested that's why poverty is spreading in the third world, the old woman wisely pretended not to hear me. And so it continued. Rui saw there was more than what he likes to call "interrupted sadness" in my face, so he started musing about life choices and the noncompulsory nature of maternity in our society. Worse still, he moved on from there to the topic of some compelling stories about transsexuals he'd seen during a television panel a few days earlier; my father-in-law was practically crawling up the walls, repeating in distress, "By the time my grandchildren are grown, it's going to be mandatory to be gay." My mother-in-law nodded and issued her own maxim: "Everybody should have a child, at least one, to support them in their old age."

I, for one, would hate to know I'd been produced as part of a retirement plan. It's at these moments that I physically feel the heat of my nonexistent father in my veins. At these moments, I love my mother's generous love with fervent faith.

These days, I feel as shocked to hear people argue for the advantages of having offspring as Rui's Grandma Marple does at hearing a woman say, "I want to advance my career. I don't have the time or the money to spend on children." The thing is, it's not a rational decision, not ever—it can't be, because, as my control-freak friend Nuno always says, a child is an uncontrollable product. Eager parents' primary mistake is to believe that a child will mean the fulfillment of their own frustrated dreams. I believe that when a person dispenses with the frenzy of pragmatic gambling in favor of platonic work, the investment almost always pays off.

A lot more is inherited than you'd think at first glance. Values, ways of feeling and expressing emotions. It's not as insignificant as it seems. My curiosity about the forms of the universe and my love for art of all kinds is rooted less in my mother's profession than in my having been trained for joy, inculcated with a notion of the world as a transformable place that's full of possibilities. That was the atmosphere I was raised in—one that was the product of not just my mother's (and father's?) blood but also your example, and even that of old Rosário, nearly illiterate but full of real delight at those little details that make life more pleasant. And it seems to me that the disenchantment of today's youth comes from the lack of those values. You always talk about Armanda's daughter, who doesn't study, doesn't work, doesn't seem to be interested in anything—much like the children of almost all my mother's friends. But those unblemished children of May 1968 grew up surrounded by people who were both terribly loud and hopelessly morose, who spent their lives clamoring that the world was lost and there was nothing to be done about it.

Rui and I die laughing at the thought that we might end up raising a soccer player or a diet-pill salesman. But I couldn't care less. I'll just try to make sure my child knows how to be happy and see everybody—from the chairman to the garbage man—as transitory people in transitory situations, just like her.

As you see, dear Jenny, I'm perfectly capable of talking about Rui after all. So much so that I almost forgot the main purpose of this letter, which is to tell you about the launch party for Delfim Veleno's book. It was really well attended, and Delfim proved to have the sort of charisma that makes people into cult figures. He showed up in a gorgeous night-blue Italian suit, a patterned silk kerchief glowing around his neck over his white shirt. Since I know you don't watch television, I'll tell you that the cameras captured him receiving an enthusiastic kiss from Glória, who appeared with her new boyfriend—that businessman, Idílio Carrasco; you must have heard about it already.

The book was introduced by Sebastião and Manuel Almada, who described it as a powerful blow against the placidity and mythos of the entertaining tales that so many people mistake for literature.

I read it in one go, Jenny. By now you must have received your copy from Delfim himself, who's completely reenergized and eager to pay you a visit. I hope you let him in instead of being so paranoid this time. *Throw Me to the Wolves* is the monologue of a man declaiming his destiny, as if by doing so he could exorcise his demons. But the desperate imperative of solitude transforms the monologue into a dialogue, a staging, a regurgitation of memories. Ângelo, the narrator, completed a philosophy degree and wrote his thesis on Plato, but, like his father before him, he ekes out a living by selling his body and shielding his soul from any hint of male compassion. He's envious of Lúcio, a sadist who apparently draws more customers. Lúcio reciprocates Ângelo's jealous admiration through a strange form of love. In short, it's a brutal exploration of the hierarchies of marginal power, a voice that resists the hatred, resignation, and madness to which history has condemned it. Veleno fled from his old bourgeois aptitudes and found the lumpenproletariat. Or, to put it another way, the light. So may you, too, be reborn. And me. I don't know why Veleno's book has filled me with this sense of impending calamity. Maybe it's nothing and my sadness is about to be, as Rui says, interrupted once more.

A big kiss from your
Natália

5

Lisbon, February 15, 1991

Dear Jenny,

I just finished another massive interior remodeling project, and I'm feeling burned out. For this one I had to convert a chapel into a nightclub with bright, colorful lights and the whole Disney family, from Uncle Scrooge to the witch from *Snow White*, parading across the walls. And put up a bunch of Greek columns "like the ones in the Acropolis" down the length of a dining room that the owners thought looked too empty. And fill all the walls with "trompe l'oeil frescos": in the boy's room, scenes from *Star Wars*, with a bed shaped like a spaceship; in the girl's room, contemporary dancers, like the ones from the TV show *Fame*; in the parents' room, an English garden full of fountains, which seemed to go with the Queen Anne furniture. At least all these murals had the benefit of padding the wallets of a number of unemployed artists.

Sílvia in particular got a lot of praise for her *Star Wars* scene, which she painted under the influence of so many hallucinogens that the clients described it as "a space wooze." Sílvia agreed, with a slow smile: "Yeah, it was a great *trip*." I don't know if it was a good idea to give her the commission. When she's out of work, Sílvia has a really hard time and does drugs. But when she does have work, it seems like she has an even harder time and ups her dose. If I try to persuade her to detox, she gets offended, makes fun of me, and starts using behind my back; she thinks she's got it all under control, that she's not addicted to anything, and she's always insisting that everybody these days takes a couple of pills to relax. "The world's a rough place," she concludes, staring at me with her beautiful, hollow eyes. "Haven't you noticed?" It's hard for me to see her like that, still in her early twenties, squandering her remarkable talents. At first, everybody, including Leonor, criticized me for offering her an internship here at Telhados de Vidro. I knew her only vaguely from evenings out; I'd seen two of her paintings in a group show and been really impressed when she showed me the work she'd done for her classes. At this point, though, nobody gets mad about her complete inability to follow a schedule or get out of bed in the mornings. Everybody—except, apparently, our reptilian secretary, Béli, who can't stand women who don't wear suits or work standard hours—supports her and cheers her on.

But our expectations are paralyzing Sílvia's talents. She'd probably welcome a little indifference. Out there, on city nights, violence undulates in deeply irrelevant waves. Despite the dead bodies, the party goes on—nobody's to blame because everybody's to blame, and unreality is eternal. Even I feel increasingly drawn to that daily escape; by the end of the day I am possessed by a vital need to forget the fake Greek columns I erect on commission in a world I'd rather make more real.

I used to define architecture as the search for amazement, which is, in turn, the touchstone of beauty. Now what amazes me is the naïveté of those definitions. I'm becoming a cynic, dear Jenny. I've swapped out all my good ideas for sarcastic comments so I don't have to admit I've given up. But it's no use proposing good ideas when my clients have got heads like a dead fish. Though at least the fish has got its mouth gaping; people can always assume it's out of surprise or fear. The fish trusted in the hook, which is a testament to its integrity.

The soundtrack to this letter I'm writing is the crabby voice of Béli, who before she became rich was named Lobélia; she's shouting at her husband over the phone because he's about to trade in their Lancia Dedra for something more practical: "That's one humiliation I refuse to put up with, do you hear me? Me, in something practical? What are people going to think? I don't care if it's Japanese. That car's a shoebox—it's humiliating." My head hurts, and Béli's voice gets on my nerves, but it's a relief to hear her. She'll call the hairdresser next to tell him she woke up with the soul of a brunette this morning and needs an appointment as soon as possible. And then the maid, to tell her to re-iron the man of the house's shirts, which are all wrinkled. And then the doctor to insist on changing her diet and exercise regimen because she's getting fat in the wrong places and her legs are still skinny.

When she hangs up, she goes back to her usual activity of sowing or irrigating gossip. Luckily, she seems to have stopped setting off wars between the people at the studio; she must have realized it was an ignoble job, unhelpful to her advancement ambitions. In any event, nobody swallows her poison anymore. Instead, she's got the accounting department in her sights. The new chief financial officer is a young man with blond hair, wide shoulders, and a square jaw topped with a promotional smile. His hobbies are tennis, jogging, and women. Whenever I go looking for him to find out why my overtime hours aren't showing up in my check, he sighs, scratches his head with his excessively perfumed fingers, stretches his neck to one side and then the other, and murmurs that he's been woolgathering because he's an incurable romantic. As far as I'm concerned, as long as he adds in the missing numbers, it makes no difference to me. I still prefer him to the previous CFO, a twitchy man with a black rug on his head who was always trying to confuse me with cryptic discussions of inputs, balances, and rates.

The new guy is having a fling with the head of the company. When they fired him from the construction company where he worked previously, he got himself introduced to our boss through a mutual friend and told her he'd been put out on the street because they suspected him of working for us as a corporate spy. It sounds unbelievable, right, Jenny? And, for precisely that reason, effective. The mutual friend, an affable young man with one of those unmemorable faces, was also working here at Telhados de Vidro. He told me he'd been struck by the blond marketer's flair for the dramatic: "They even insinuated I was your lover, just imagine. It's enormously difficult to tell you all this. But I have nothing else to lose at this point, so I wanted to at least meet the woman I was supposed to be spying for." It actually seems fitting, Jenny, that women's liberation is becoming a fantastic spring-board for men. Or at least some of them, because, as you can imagine (or maybe can't even imagine . . .), the employee who kindly made this introduction between the blond gymnast and my boss saw his own services dispensed with in the meantime . . . as a cost-saving measure.

The poetic part of this hyperrealistic tale is that the boss is actually in love with the blond adman. She's in her late forties, firm, flirtatious, and emaciated, with an inexplicable terror of cats. Her husband traded her in a few years back for a less wrinkled facsimile. After this event she went man-crazy and slightly out of control, like a teenage girl. She often comes down to the studio to discuss men's quirks, especially the way they don't like literally sleeping with women once they've succeeded in getting them into bed. Early on, the men at the studio would blush. She'd show up, lean her bony elbows on one of their drawing boards, and ask, "Listen, is it normal for a man to seduce a woman and then hop up at three in the morning to call her a taxi?" Those questions elicited a tame mixture of derision and tenderness. Now everyone is gentle with her, their compassion anticipating the pain the financial blond is going to cause her when he finds a bed better suited to his upwardly mobile objectives.

In the meantime, Rui is still in Coimbra and I've lost the habit of eating at home. I work late, go out to eat with friends, and then go on to Frágil, where I stay till I'm dazed with drowsiness. I'm attempting to rediscover the delight of my youthful nights out, but it seems like the world is out of surprises.

Last night everybody was in an uproar because a man had gone into an eatery out in the countryside and started shooting. He killed six people and then himself. "Finally. It's a sign Portugal's becoming part of civilization," said Vítor, who's a rock critic and likes having cutting-edge, original thoughts. "Too bad it's the only sign," his wife commented; her name is Isménia and she's a fashion designer. "Actually, the United States is in complete decline. In terms of fashion, it's over. All they care about is selling things. Maybe serial killers are the only truth that's really possible. The only ones who are actually pure." Isménia is a big fan of purity. She quit smoking, dumped the cocaine, started lifting weights and stretching. She can't stand fabrics that wrinkle, like linen, or that can't go in the washing machine, like silk. She works with body-hugging microfibers, spandexes, and Lycras. She's preparing her first men's collection, combating unisex banality with garments that highlight men's masculine qualities and herald what she calls twenty-first-century masculinity, inspired by Marlon Brando in *A Streetcar Named Desire*. But more glamorous.

Nuno, who gave up painting and architecture to start a public relations company, said that serial killers at least spare us the morality charade. "There's nothing more boring than a criminal with motives, feelings, and honor. Things are always going to be simpler and more straightforward," Nuno said.

There are no noble crimes anymore for the simple reason that nobility is, first and foremost, a way to orchestrate time. Or it was: meanwhile, time changed its gender and its speed and became pure velocity. It seems the criminal world doesn't have room for contemplative ecstasy or aesthetic games either. They kill the way they live: pragmatic, swift. Today, where would one go to find those artists of assassination, those calm, cultured, indifferent souls who made the fortune of Philo Vance, the erudite detective born of the pen of S. S. Van Dine? These days nobody even kills out of desire, jeopardizing their soul—risking guilt and remorse. They kill because it's part of the routine, like a trip to the dentist.

And they choose ever more efficient and less romantic tactics, making people's evil sides shine ever more brightly: a gunshot in the dark, some dollar bills, a stealthy stabbing. Hypothesis: nobody is entirely to blame and nobody should devote all his energy to anything, because disappointment is inevitable. Free yourselves of passion; trample on idealism or be trampled yourselves. That was more or less what I said, and Nuno nodded: "Right. Everything's much clearer now. At least nobody's hiding behind that sentimental fakery."

Something inside me always shrinks when I return to my empty house, the beat of the music and the clinking of ice in the glasses still ringing in my ears. I can't even manage to miss Rui; I like knowing he and his emphatic optimism exist somewhere out there. But it's a place to visit, not one where my life can reside.

A somewhat lost kiss from your
Natália

6

Lisbon, August 15, 1991

Dear Jenny,

I just got home from visiting you and I wanted to write to you, I don't know why. I'd have liked to stay with you a little longer today, but when Manuel Almada came in I felt like I should leave the two of you alone. It's not that we have secrets. Actually, this sharing of Manuel's friendship functions as a sort of secret between us. We are very alike in this way, carrying on friendship through an absolutely private dialogue. We cultivate social circles as if they were impressionist paintings; from a distance they're blue-tinted images of unwavering harmony, and up close they're saturated blotches of color, individual scintillations that exist outside of any design. I am certain that Manuel never tells you anything about my life, because he's never told me anything about yours.

I confess I once asked him if you'd thought Grandpa Tó Zé and Grandpa Pedro's extreme devotion to each other was normal. And said that sometimes it seemed to me their relationship had the same sort of tragic quality that love does. Manuel smiled and answered with another question: "Love, friendship, what do they mean? They're just conventions, my dear. People love each other or they don't. And there are different ways of expressing that emotion, which change over time. The thing is, your family is made up of people with great intensity. They are able to endure emotions that last, with all their internal imbalances, an entire lifetime. There aren't many people like that. There never were. That's why I'm so fond of you. Because you honor that legacy in your heart."

Dear Jenny, you can't imagine how embarrassed I was by those words. I felt the rafters of the theater of vices that my eschatological mind had constructed crashing down on my head, one by one. I felt guilty, even more so than during Grandpa Tó Zé's long decline, three years ago now, as you and Grandpa Pedro prayed at his bedside, dripping beads of water onto his lips with a sponge. He was no longer able to eat or drink; we couldn't even tell if he was still lucid. I remember how you hugged and kissed Grandpa Pedro with great urgency, promising that Grandfather Tó Zé had passed to the other side, to a place without suffering. And I remember how, a year later, Grandpa Pedro died of loneliness and longing. My mother and I visited him every other day. We tried several times to bring him home with us, but he said that at least he could see the Tagus where he was. The nurses told us they'd never seen anything like it, a person deteriorating without any biological cause. I'm sitting by the window as I write, Jenny, and the water of the Tagus, dotted with white ferries, makes up for the emptiness that spreads along the walls of my house. I got married two years ago, and the art is still stacked up on the living room floor. The lace towel you made me has never been used. We didn't buy a table or chairs for the living room, and the housewarming dinner we promised our friends has been postponed indefinitely. We never had time. And I don't think we're going to have the patience to have it anytime soon.

It's a good thing I put my foot down on the river view. Rui used to say it was a bit of romantic foolishness, that the river was going to cost us an arm and a leg. But I was bound and determined to find a view at a good price, and I did. At first, my husband said he refused to climb five flights of stairs without an elevator just to enjoy the view. But my mind was made up, and my silent determination always wins out over his animated arguing in the end. We're like the sun and the wind from that La Fontaine fable. I was certain I was going to rent this house even before I saw it. The landlady opened the door, looked me up and down, and said she'd just rented it out half an hour earlier. I insisted, and she repeated that there was no point. I went down the stairs in a fury, called Rui, and told him I had to see him immediately. I made him go up on his own. The landlady showed him the apartment and told him she'd be delighted to close the deal with him.

I'll never forget the look on the woman's face when Rui returned with me. She started stammering excuses, rubbing her greasy hands on her flowered robe. She said the first renter had called just five minutes after I'd left to say he didn't want the house after all. She'd even gone to the window to call after me, hoping I was still in earshot. Poor thing. Her soft face was drooping toward her trembling shoulders as she desperately apologized. Her small eyes rolled wildly, still stunned by the sudden discovery that a biracial woman in jeans could turn out to be a successful architect.

I'm exhausted by conversations about race. At cocktail parties and gallery openings, when people find themselves with a drink in their hand and nothing else to do, they come up to me and ask if I'm from Cape Verde and then start telling stories about discrimination in a shocked tone. For a while I thought that was making my life easier because, as Manuel Almada would say, it helped me thin my crop of potential suitors: anybody who mentioned my skin color was automatically eliminated. Now, though, I cut them right off. As soon as anyone starts in on the topic, I grin and produce this lethal observation: "Well, the problem is that the people who propagate racism do it every day. But the people who condemn it are only looking for an explanation. They don't do anything about it every day. It's easy to talk about it; fighting it is a little more complicated." That always makes them go pale, Jenny. Like fish out of water.

The swath of river that's visible from here is completely different from the bit I used to contemplate from the balconies of Chess House. From here I see the Cais das Colunas instead of the bridge and the statue of Christ the King. But the cold blue of the water, despite Heraclitus's protestations, is the same. The light dances in waves on the movement of the boats. In the middle of the night the glowing vessels cry out, filling the voids of absence between dreams. Those horns soothe me, as if they were confirming the roundness of the earth and the futility of fretting.

I saw Álvaro yesterday. That's what I was about to tell you when Manuel Almada arrived. Around dinnertime I was working with Leonor at the studio and suddenly felt a throbbing in the back of my neck, as if a ball of fire were slowly rising up my spine. And at that moment I somehow knew that Álvaro was at the Quarteto Cinema. Don't ask me how. It's as if some murky messenger had written a telegram on my nerves: *Álvaro. Quarteto.* I hadn't been to the movies in ages, and I hadn't seen Álvaro since I kicked him out of my wedding, totally drunk. I grabbed Leonor by the arm and said, "Let's go to the Quarteto. Right now." She asked me what movies were playing, what the rush was. I told her it didn't matter, that I was wiped out and was suddenly craving a slice of the Quarteto's sponge cake. As you know, I've never believed in premonitions. Álvaro was sitting on the balcony of the café, drinking coffee and eating a slice of sponge cake. He spoke to me calmly, as if we'd last seen each other just yesterday. We went into the theater together and I sat beside him. I don't remember a thing about the movie except that it was about the mafia and a lot of people died. From time to time Leonor got scared and grabbed my hand. My hands were sweaty and I felt naked, completely exposed. Álvaro's motionless body kept giving off floods of a glimmering scent that made me tremble to my core, like a gust of fever. When the movie ended he practically ran off, saying he had to get up early because he was leaving for Brussels the next day. He didn't ask about Rui. I ended up going out for a drink at the Pavilhão Chinês with Leonor, who spent an hour talking about how hypothetical people need to shed their hang-ups and look inside themselves, and recognize their true soul mates. I think she must be in love, but I wasn't in the mood to get into it.

In the meantime, Rui put off our vacation for the third time, and I was relieved. Increasingly, I long to return to Africa. Any part of Africa, even if it can't be Mozambique. But I want to go alone. Or at least I want to go without Rui—who knows why. My mother suggested that I go with her and Armanda and her daughter to southern Greece, but I didn't feel like that either. I like Lisbon in the summertime—everything slows down and spreads out. Besides, don't tell my mother, but I find it pathetic, if not depressing: a group of single women stalking Mediterranean lovers on the beach.

Sometimes I start thinking maybe he's having an affair up there in Coimbra. That he's got what you would call a lover. I know him well enough to know that, however much his career means to him and however thrilling he finds saving lives, his thirst for experience is not the sort that can be quenched by work alone. And women always see a doctor as a lustful god, and he knows it. Especially a surgeon—even if he's just a resident at the moment. I, too, was fascinated by the idea of making love with a man who could shape my body with a scalpel, my very core, down to the bone. I succumbed to the erotic of dismemberment, which flourishes as an insidious counterpoint to women's independence. Men tend to femininize themselves in their effort to support our slog toward emancipation: they weep with us, they burn themselves on frying pans with us, they sweat by our side in the gym mirrors. And we find ourselves dreaming of a man with icy eyes, one who treats us like soulless bodies with all the forbidden refinements. For a long time I thought my dreams of submission had to do with my father's absence. For a long time I thought a lot. Álvaro was the only person who could make me stop thinking. Actually, it was only after Álvaro that I learned to play doctor. And I'm getting fed up with playing. And with thinking, which is the same thing.

A dazed kiss from your
Natália

7

Lisbon, December 9, 1991

Dear Jenny,

I quit smoking six years ago because of her. Actually, to be precise, I should say I decided to quit smoking because of me, but I never would have pulled it off without her support. She gave me a gift for every week I went without cigarettes. And whenever temptation reared its head, I'd focus on a fantasy in which an evil man would start torturing her as soon as I flicked my lighter. Or that there was a bomb in her house that would go off. I managed to carry on with this childish story till the end because Leonor was the protagonist. I like every version of her—even if I've always been irritated by a certain authoritarian inclination that occasionally comes over her. But my own ill temper and cruelty irritate me too—I just try not to take them too far, and only part time. And Leonor was also the one who taught me to laugh at myself.

Dear Jenny, friends are the only compelling hypothesis for how a person can manage to survive childhood. And now I think I've lost my best friend. She's been abducted by that dragon we encounter in adulthood, sex. Maybe I'm simplifying too much. I always try to explain everything. I'm one of those "civilized" people who swap out the blind courage of living for the fantasy of thinking. "Has it ever occurred to you that thinking too much might make you just as dumb as thinking too little?" Leonor asked me, devastated. I had just told her that a romantic relationship with a woman was completely unthinkable for me.

It happened last Sunday. We were sitting by the brazier with tea, scones, and our newest projects on the table, delighted with the keening of the wind and the rain lashing at the windows. On the television they were showing a documentary, *Reconstructive Plastic Surgery for Battered Women*, and a sociologist was explaining that the nuclear family is disappearing because it has served people poorly.

Suddenly Leonor, conventional, diplomatic Leonor, grabbed my face with her fingers pressed tight together and declared, "I love you. I can't live without you." Before I even had time to breathe, she kissed me so fiercely that she cut my lip. I tried to make a joke of it; I went back to our old black slave routine, said my white mistress was bewitched or something like that, and she called me stupid and mean, her voice rough. Then she cried. And I tried to explain. And she told me, "I feel sorry for you, shutting yourself off with reasons and explanations. I know your deepest self, and I know it's larger and broader than that." I felt bad for all the times I'd told her I wished I was as pretty as she. I felt bad for the intense pleasure it gave me to brush her silky hair. But most of all I felt bad for having provoked that look of desolate scorn in her eyes with this crude statement: "I didn't know you liked women." "Well, now you do," she replied. Now I knew she was as capable of loving women as she was men and dogs and birds. "There are no limits on liking, sweetie. But of course you yuppies are so obsessed with physicality that you can't like people that way."

Love defies explanation, doesn't it, Jenny? Your love for António, his love for Pedro. Love doesn't give a fig about our ideas about our own identities or sexual preferences. Biological sex is an accident that is irrelevant to passion's obstinate intentions. My love for Leonor, Leonor's love for me—I see them now as stars passing each other on the vast emptiness of a firmament made of blue construction paper. Two scattered vibrations of the same futile light, tracing brief, fiery trajectories across an incombustible sky.

On Monday Leonor called in sick, and I haven't heard from her in a week. I can't sleep. I wander the Lisbon dawn, sit outside her house staring at her glowing window, smoking in the car. I'm tempted to ring the doorbell for my own reassurance, but the idea that it might upset her even more stops my hand. At any moment, I think, a flicker of telepathy will drive her downstairs to find me. Lisbon at four in the morning is still the same as my old Leonor—the new avenues with those sulfurous lights that illuminate the night without extinguishing its melancholy air, enough for us to feel safe and cozy while still reminding us of the movies we see today and the ones we used to see in the past. Time and time again I would awaken Leonor in the middle of the night so she could bind the wounds that Álvaro insisted on continually reopening. What reconstructive surgery can there be for today's high-powered women, who don't allow themselves to be battered but allow their hearts to be sliced in two?

I often attract people I do not like. It is stressful to cast aside the gallant solicitations I unwillingly provoke, in an eddy of politeness that sooner or later inspires the viscous melody of resentment. I am nice on principle, a principle that is actually quite amoral. No preselection. I find a stone for my buildings in every voice. I grew up in that era when concrete came to be appreciated as much as marble, and all hierarchies merged into a cyclical harmony of injustice. Back in our university days, my friend Nuno used to organize his address book according to what he called "areas of sentimental exploration": under A, he included the names of his friends who would accompany him on artistic outings; under B, the ones who were good for bars and benders; under S, the ones who could help him along on his way to success; under T, those who'd enjoy a night at the theater; and under X, those rare few who could serve multiple purposes. I was fascinated by his unique method, and it made me be even nicer. I was trying to create a world without waste. Nothing is lost, everything transforms.

The approach worked. I earned good grades, earned a spot at a good studio. I also acquired a reputation as someone who could salvage foundering projects, which at first suited me quite well. But one day I noticed I'd stopped being given exciting projects. All I was doing was restoring ruined attempts at faithfulness, giving the appearance of beauty to buildings that had been sketched, resketched, and gradually affronted. Decoration, as Álvaro said, that had no ambition to perceive anything. I specialize in enduring misunderstandings. People love me badly. They give me exactly the same kind of love I give to the things I architect: a false, fragile love that makes an impression on the retina at first impact but then becomes unbearable. People love me beside me. Despite me. I think only Álvaro and Leonor have managed to love me in the raw, in the beauty that exists beyond me. I don't know how I can live without another pair of eyes to reflect back that interior crystal that does not sparkle at me in mirrors.

Leonor always came to class late that autumn I met her, her eyes swollen with sleep, garbed in a brown cloak that covered her down to her feet and, fluttering with her bouncing steps, made her look like a squirrel. She would sit down and stick her hand in the air, almost automatically: "I don't understand, Professor. Would you mind explaining it again?" Over the years she resigned herself to being punctual, learned to diet, and shed the squirrel cloak. Thanks to those transformations that rounded off her angular interiors and flattened her facade, people started to like her. I continued to like her as if nothing had changed. Despite what they say, feelings don't change all that much. They're born old; they cling to your guts like an illness and their smell lingers after their death. That's why nobody likes feelings anymore. They don't go with the walls of this era. They don't go anywhere. They don't evolve.

Leonor never wanted to be an artist. She always used to say, in a decided tone, that she had no talent and was instead motivated by the pursuit of knowledge. One day she told Sebastião Lucas, "Fundamentally, I'm like you. You know everything about how a novel should be written, but you don't know how to write. Only difference is I don't want to know everything about anything." These statements swept the room like a tornado of insolence. From Sebastião the socialist to Isménia the designer, everybody asked me what I saw in her.

What I see in her, Jenny, like what I see in you, is a summation of tiny details that stretches toward infinity. A summation in which her upturned nose is as invaluable as her loyalty. Her straightforward attitude is as beautiful as her large hands with their square fingernails. Beauty does not exist outside the intimacy of contemplation, nor can it forcibly set aglow a self-evidently lovely face. That's why I'm disgusted by today's adolescent obsession with attracting counterparts that resemble oneself, or, equivalently, one's opposite.

It doesn't matter what emphasis you give, what words you use, what support you offer—all of that is as far removed from the cold passion of love as the faux Greek columns I design are from the real Greece. In the same way, Leonor is, for me, the shadow of Álvaro's definitive reality, even if they are outwardly of different genders. The indomitable chill of ardor casts its icy shadow, to the detriment of the workings of affection, sex, and justice in the world.

A possibly enamored kiss from your
Natália

8

Lisbon, December 28, 1993

Dear Jenny,

You carried my marriage with you into death. On the day of your funeral, I used the strength of the tears you left me to tell Rui that it was all over between us. He didn't listen. He kept stroking my hair with that clinical skill of his that sometimes hypnotized me. I said it again: "It's all over, Rui." He said, "OK, OK, don't get worked up," and started massaging the back of my neck. Rui thought all my problems could be solved that way: "OK, OK." A simple pirouette, an efficient manipulation of the fingers, and that was that. Apparently it took your dying for me to realize it. When they shut the door of your mausoleum, I felt as if they were shutting the doors of fear in my soul.

All the mistakes on earth can be summed up with this blunt phrase: life avoidance. We know that life itself will inexorably take care to avoid us, and yet we refuse to follow the unique music of our blood, even at the end. Your death, Jenny, points to the proximity of my own. It was terrifying to think that one of these days I will cease to exist, leaving nothing but an "OK, OK" to remember me by. Even more terrifying was the thought that there might be a sky onto which a life's essence is projected in CinemaScope, a sky from which the lives that never dared to unfold sprinkle like a light rain onto the ignorance of the living.

Rui and I fell into that most common of romantic errors: treating affections like architecture projects or babies. In love, whether it's linked to sex (passion) or everyday life (marriage) or elective affinities (friendship), what we call instruction is actually desensitization and forgetting, strategies for surviving the absolute that impels us toward the final fusion.

I ended up having to tell Rui I was in love with another man. That was the only way I could get him to pay attention, to believe me. He couldn't accept being dumped of his own doing, much less mine. I was his natural complement, the successful accessory to his success. I didn't tell him that I don't even know if Álvaro is going to want me. I didn't tell him I'm not afraid of being alone. That would give him hope, inspire him to engage in an agonizing, futile attempt at reconquest, which he doesn't deserve. Rui said he understood, caressed me slowly, his fingers shaking this time, not the least bit clinical. He didn't shed a tear or voice any objection. He just said he'd move out. I insisted that I should be the one to move out, but he said he couldn't live there without me. Then he wordlessly packed his suitcases and left, patting me on the cheek. Dear Jenny, I had thought the shining shadow cast by your life would make my new skin glow. You used to say that pain is a bonus bit of wisdom left to us by happiness. So why is it so hard to bear?

These months have been painful ones, Jenny, a slow, suffocated pain, without any discernable grandeur. Love affairs, which dispense with the world and all its inhabitants—the beloved doesn't count, having fallen to Earth from another planet—attract endless lists of supporters, euphoric pages of signatories. Breakups never confront such activists. A divorce is a triple somersault, a triply "deadly leap," in slow motion. Everything dies in us: the other person, that other half of us that belongs to the other, the stable image that the people around us had of our relationship. And it all dies slowly, with sobs, without funeral rites or mourning ceremonies. There are no flowers or tears or prayers or eulogies; the burial of those who once pledged eternal love takes place in a courtroom, the realm of crime and guilt, of punishments that placate the collective conscience.

The judge shuffles his papers, asks, eyeing the clock, if we want to "change our minds," and sets the next hearing. Out in the hallway young ex-couples are being shepherded in an endless line by lawyers almost as young as them, sort of posthumous chaperones, who are describing their most spectacular cases to dissipate the tension. There's one lawyer per couple; it will be their last shared expense. That's how mutual consent divorces are carried out, in an affable tone and for an affordable price. It's no longer something that only happens to other people, but the new banality of the process only strips it more thoroughly of dignity: a divorcing couple increases the statistics on human precarity, bolsters claims of the decay of fundamental values, and rouses paternalistic skepticism.

Our friends, who humbly applauded and admired the birth of our love, suddenly become wise, omniscient, professorial: either they foresaw everything and try to present detailed evidence that apparently only we failed to see, or they hadn't foreseen a thing and cover their faces in horror at our childish thoughtlessness. They rarely resist the temptation to identify a victim and a tormentor, to console one or excuse the other with well-intentioned recriminations that only pour salt in the wound. It's nobody's fault; the heart, moving from blackness to blackness, remains on the margins of the law of sin and redemption. Still remaining are the day-to-day laws of this marriage, which were drawn up and ratified in an unobserved, intimate way that is now being broadcast, as things come to an end, like an inviolable secret.

These gray, shadowy days infiltrate my work too. The administrator has become a pyre of fury ever since the handsome head accountant, through his customary methods, went off to become the deputy director of an advertising agency. The first consequence of his departure was that the administrator established quotas. Whereas previously we had worked long hours to justify Telhados de Vidro's good reputation, we were now prodded to produce in order to justify our hours. The second consequence was that we ended up without a CFO: the administrator is taking on more and more roles and has started talking about layoffs. She harangues people about incompetence and competitiveness, issuing thinly veiled threats.

Dear Jenny, why do we neglect the fuses of our heart and allow the black fog of resentment to invade the clarity of our blood? We insist on applying the gears of power—which, like anything made of iron that inhabits the realm of oxygen, are perishable—to our emotions, which bear the same luminous wake as oft-navigated seas. At worst, slavery; at best, dissolution—we call these postmilitary dictatorships eternal love, and so, brimming with martyrdom, we find consolation in the notion that we are true angels of goodness, souls made vast by suffering.

Without the solace of these divine trumpets, the situation tends to degenerate; we love humanity as a whole, which tends to be insipid and ungrateful; unwittingly, we major in minor perfidies. Having acquired a taste for it, we go on to pursue a doctorate in complex revenge techniques, and our life is transformed into a childish game of the terribly dangerous variety, with anonymous letters and concealed trapdoors. And that's where my sweet Leonor is now: she's adopted Buddhism, dresses all in white, leaves flowers on everybody's drawing boards, went vegetarian to free herself from the violence of meat, and also disguises her handwriting to write me letters signed by "a friend" that describe Rui's adulteries or, more recently, Álvaro's alleged kissing-and-telling about me. But her fake handwriting wavers as it issues from the nib of her unmistakable fountain pen, revealing the stifled rebellion within that hand that pretends so poorly. And when by chance her eyes meet mine, I read in them the dull sense of guilt that we call remorse. Clearly, Jenny, I don't know how to create intimacy with women. As proof, consider this: the only one I managed to do it with fell in love with me.

Manuel Almada says we're in the prehistory of love, and he's more and more right all the time. There are still very few people who can bear testimony to the first of Christ's precepts: love your neighbor as yourself. It seems that even self-love melts away under the growing attachments of the body and the galloping social competition we insist on calling *life*. We bring with us the weight of an entire millennium and the speed of a lightning century. Jenny, you used to say that as we moved into the new era, love would punt power and its strategies—which were deadly to the point of absurdity—to the ends of the galaxy. Manuel would smile melancholically and say nothing. I wanted to believe with you in time's capacity for regeneration, but now that you're dead I don't know anymore. Time wasn't even able to carry you into the twenty-first century.

Even so, I know I'm not going to give up the intense, slow flavor of love. I can't. It would be an insult to the memory of my blood that is made of the stuff of yours. I used to be afraid of love, Jenny, but at the moment of your death, I felt that I was inheriting your courage. I felt that you were shedding your skin so that I could put it on, and I found in it once more the amalgam of my trampled dreams. Your death has brought back my passion, isolated from the apparatuses of mobility, preserved in the static fire that defines immortal things, immune to the vanities of time and the human efforts of evolution.

But now everything is dimming in my memory; *remember* is the dizzying declension of the verb *forget*. Surrounded by judges and accountants but somehow on our own, Rui and I look at each other like old lovers, trying to discover what elements in our respective souls (how strange, suddenly having a soul that is mine alone, dark and silent) are mobile or immobile, what in our own bodies we have forgotten, learned, learned to forget, forgotten to learn. Rui is talking quickly: he doesn't want his sadness to have time to settle among his words. Justice is imposed like an absurd law, an external truth, a curtain made of smoke that we draw between us and the cruelty of our emotions, which cannot be resolved through the democratic efficacy of sharing.

There is no sharing in marriage: there is fusion, commingling, dilution of the self in the golden circle of a wedding band; we allow the name that gleams inside it to shield us from all vertigo, protect us from all our nightmarish secrets. I remember how I used to wake him at dawn, excited and insecure, so he could approve my latest project. I remember the codfish with cream sauce that he made better than anyone. I remember the cold blue days on which we discovered Paris, hand in hand. Probably only people who stubbornly insist on pushing their bond to the limits of authenticity end up divorcing, only those who have the courage to look each other in the eye and find that yesterday's love deserves more than the comfort of habit and the conformism of complementarity. Only those who can't bear discovering that they are still themselves, now faded with the passing years, after having grown, in the dazzling lucidity of love, so much together.

Divorce can be an act of radical, absolute union, a binding together for eternity of two souls who once loved each other too much to be able to love each other in another manner, one that is small and gentle, almost vegetal. A halted embrace outside of time, which tightens in the moment of its disappearance, before the world's very eyes, because it goes beyond the predefined models of war and peace. A final desire for immortality, which lights up the night where all desires would seem to be sleeping the sleep of the righteous and the fulfilled.

Having been lovers for years, we now rediscover ourselves, stunned, soaring above the melancholy of our shared past and the abyss of our solitary future. Only the two of us know that it's not a question of success or failure. Only we know that what we are feeling has no remedy—and it is in the name of that irremediable something that used to make us tremble that we are now separating. Beyond the injury of our days, of the books, records, and movies that gave our life color, we find ourselves now immersed together in the trauma of suffering, this absence from each other as we now no longer remember having been in each other's presence. It's an unfeasible form of love that, as such, has no end.

An infinite kiss from your
Natália

9

Maputo, June 21, 1994

Dear Jenny,

The very first letter I'm writing from this land that shelters my father's corpse is to a dead woman. I should have written to my mother, but words were always a complicated business between the two of us. I need to be holding her hands when I tell her everything I've been learning about my father here. I thought all I'd have to do was land in Mozambique to find the shadow of the unknown soldier who unwittingly gave me his blood. That's what I thought, but these things don't happen by virtue of thinking. At night I lean out over the vastness of the sea, stare up at the full moon, which is much larger here than it is in Portugal, and call to him. He doesn't answer, not even the hint of an echo. Dear Jenny, search for him in the corners of your heaven, ask him to descend on the warm night breeze into the silence of my heart. Ask him to waft a word to me, just one, that I can say to him.

It was because of him that I immediately accepted the invitation to participate in this cooperative project rebuilding bombed schools. Well, it was because of me too. Which is ultimately the same thing.

I never dreamed so much suffering was possible. Mozambique's everyday existence is practically unimaginable. When you first arrive, as you stare out through the car windows, Maputo looks like the capital of a possible future that has been shelved, a suspended experience shrouded in the crumbling colors of an unreal past. When you stop to look closer, the romantically surreal cityscape takes on the hellish contours of hyperreality.

At first glance I thought it was a heap of rags there under the store's neon sign across from the ministry building, but that would be strange in a city where garbage never piles up because anything you leave outside always has some value for somebody else. A piece of tatty wool clothing with a hole in the collar can be turned into an undershirt; a chair with missing legs can be used to block the wind or as kindling for a fire; the shoes that are superfluous for a foot that was blown to bits by a mine can serve the next person who steps onto that same ground after it has been restored to innocence. At night in Maputo all the heaps of rags have people inside them, often former soldiers, just ten or twelve years old, who were recruited at five into FRELIMO's army, or RENAMO's—makes no difference which—and who were shooting to kill from the time they were eight.

When I approached, the heap of rags stirred. The bodies lying underneath were four or six years of age

and serenely asleep; the ones on top looked like teen-
agers and were carefully hunting through anything
resembling a pocket on those poor human mattresses,
looking for money. I found myself scolding them:
"Aren't you ashamed to rob younger kids?" One of
them smiled and started explaining that he'd been
robbed when he was younger too, saying we have to
share, look after one another; food doesn't just appear
out of nowhere—he must have spent some time in a
shelter for street kids and learned that justifying your
actions will always get you further. Then they demand
dollars, meticals, or cigarettes.

Everything has a price, but life after war doesn't
seem to be worth much. Television programs feed
off of quick blood; people are moved by flamboy-
ant poverty, swollen-bellied hunger, pyrotechnics.
In Mozambique, at least for the moment, the show's
over; Rwanda's lights are glowing brighter now, so
that's where the box office sales have headed.

A week ago I flew to the city of Beira. You
wouldn't even see that level of destruction after a
hostile Martian invasion; decay had contaminated
the very air the city was breathing. You can't breathe
freely, not even at the seashore: the stench of the trash
heaps ringing the elegant homes in the Marginal
neighborhood overpowers the ocean breeze. Any object, any creature that moves is immediately carried
off by swarms of flies. Afterward, I traveled the famous Beira corridor, which served as a safe haven for
thousands of refugees.

We stopped in a village built in 1987 by more
than four hundred families fleeing from the war. The

people there were dying in droves, slowly, every day: dysentery, malaria, diarrhea, conjunctivitis, measles. The reason is simple: the river isn't flowing, so the stagnant waters are full of disease. They'd dug a well and found water but had been waiting for a pump for six months. In the meantime, people were dying. Of disease, of hunger, of everything. But the men sitting in the doors of their huts would smile, say, "Thank you" and "Welcome." That's all the Portuguese they know, but they like to talk. You hardly saw the women: they'd be in the *machambas*, which is what they call vegetable gardens in Mozambican Portuguese. The women's role is to work the earth, cook, and raise the children. The men take care of the rest—basically, these days, thinking and overseeing the work.

One of them, for example, was helping his two wives knead the wet earth with their feet to make bricks for the wall of his hut. Two or three wives is standard: once the *machamba* given as the first wife's dowry isn't enough to support all the children (the average woman has seven), marriage with a second is arranged, which has to be approved by the first. The local big shot has six wives, each with her own hut, all surrounding the husband's.

The women are the ones who walk along the roadsides carrying tree trunks on their heads, almost all of them with babies on their backs. In the luckiest villages not even their arms go to waste: the women transport all the water too. In Mavalane, a suburb of Maputo, they organized a campaign to end crime, which was robbing them of their resources. The women built a school, a carpentry shop, a soap factory, and a shoe repair shop with their own hands. At first the neighbors scoffed, but in fact, crime rates did fall. I still remember the happiness flooding one very young woman's face as she told me, while breastfeeding the youngest of her five children, "You have to believe the best of people. Otherwise, if everyone just looks out for himself, that's not really living, is it?" It's moments like these, phrases that seem to have been pulled from a human bible that precedes the avarice of time, that binds foreigners to Africa, in an instant and eternally.

Maybe that's the meaning of it all. Something made of light, bigger than all the little circumstances of the heart. That something is equally present in the actions of that illiterate mother; in those of Enrique Querol, an Argentine ex-revolutionary I met when he was running the Red Cross in Chimoio; and in those of José Maria, a Catholic missionary. "We are inheritors of ruins," he used to say, looking over at Nelson, who went out in uniform to kill people, and in that moment he looked like a soccer star glowing before a crowd of survivors. Yes, I too am an inheritor of ruins. But a wealthy heiress, unacquainted with the beginning or end of her inheritance. Out of nowhere, I decided to go to Feitor Praça, or what was left of it; I mustered the courage to face the specter of my father's torture.

Half of the country's schools were simply destroyed. Traveling south through the districts of Macia and Xai-Xai, I passed an endless series of disemboweled buildings, houses with the faint memory of their original blues, pinks, or yellows still clinging to the stone, now roofless ghosts, full of silent children. I searched for my father's breathing. Had he been one of these boys, back in that mythical time of walls and roofs?

Classes had started up again, but there was no laughter, not a pin dropping in the gentle melancholy. The rain beat soft, softly, and, at the teacher's encouragement, the children repeated in a slow chorus, "Good morning, esteemed visitors." The war created new distances, transformed communities' geographies; in improvised villages in the middle of nowhere, families worked hard to guarantee their children's academic survival, hiring teachers and setting up a system of community schools. That's what people say, at least, but there's no way to describe it in practice: To get there you have to travel for hours on end through grasses and groves. Then, in a best-case scenario, you find one or two huts that are slightly larger than the ones used as dwellings, full of barefoot children sitting in an orderly fashion on tree trunks arranged on the dirt floor, wearing rags at best, holding beat-up notebooks and little stubs of pencil in their hands. You can recognize the teachers because they're standing in front of the class, they're a bit older than the students, and sometimes they're wearing shoes of some kind. On occasion there's a broken piece of blackboard and a stub of chalk.

They use the arithmetic of sticks and pebbles: What's three plus four? Immediately, almost all of them raise their hands—they want to come to the board to show off, and when they get there they start dividing up the sticks and counting on their fingers. Even if they don't know the answer, it's worth it because it's fun, a novelty, and they get to be in a photograph. We stopped at a dozen of these schools, and at all of them the principal would bustle out to bless the journey of the school inspector who was with us, begging him for notebooks, textbooks, pencils, teacher training, more frequent visits. At first glance they seem alive. Then you note their stillness, see that they don't know what to do when they're not being given orders. They don't know how to play.

I stayed one night on the beach at Xai-Xai, in the little hotel where my father unknowingly gave me to my mother. I spent a sleepless night listening to the booming waves, waiting for a sign that never came. I got up early, quizzed the manager, the employees, the men dozing in the shadows of the palm trees, showed his photograph, but nobody remembered Xavier. As I was leaving one of the countless community schools in the Xai-Xai district, the barefoot principal had run up to give me an orange tree: "It's to bring you happiness. The kind of happiness that we enjoy." I planted the orange tree next to the little beachside hotel in Xai-Xai. In case my father appeared.

Tell him for me, Jenny, tell him these stories of his country because I don't know how. My father died for a dream of freedom. The Marxist state swapped out the all-powerful witch doctors for zealous bureaucrats, and purification ceremonies for committee meetings. Now psychologists are discovering that once children are "purified" by witch doctors, who bring the community together to chase off the evil spirit that forced the children to kill their family members, they no longer pee the bed, have nightmares, or draw villages engulfed in flames. The boys had been forced to kill their own families, the girls to sell their bodies. They'd been mutilated from the age of five to force them to obey. That's how war was waged in Mozambique after independence.

I traveled through the ravaged country on the eve of the first free elections, following the track of those who have exchanged the comforts of the West for the luxurious joy of sparking life in the dull eyes of Africa's children. Working here is deeply fulfilling, if torturous. There is an excess of miseries and a perpetual shortage of resources or any way to apply them; the Marxist bureaucracy has only intensified colonial servility. At the same time, though, there is a palpable immovable force, the strange gift of a certain virginal quality behind the Mozambicans' wounded eyes. And there is, in this devastated people that speaks close to thirty different languages, an immense capacity for healing. The Portuguese language of domination, for example, was translated into the fluid language of national unity.

I often recall these lines from Mia Couto, which I underlined in red in my copy of *Estórias Abensonhadas*: "Pain is a road: we walk the length of it to reach another place. And that place is a part of ourselves that we have never visited."

Cholera, bloody diarrhea, dysentery. Outside the capital city these words were repeated in a monotone—people had grown used to them. The heat rose with a drilling sound inside my head. Near the ruins of Feitor Praça, in a little hamlet with half a dozen huts, the women shouted and chanted rhythmically around the dead body of a fifteen-year-old girl who'd been found in a hut holding her baby, suffocated by roundworms.

"Our Father, who art in heaven . . ." I waited till the end of the mass, hunkering in the scrub, holding the battered photo of my father. Nobody remembered Xavier Sandramo. Nobody wanted to remember anything. They didn't like my intrusive, inquiring fingers on the photo. My guide and interpreter kept telling me to be patient, not to jump to my question so quickly, to ease into it. After a while the children responded to jokes and candy. Then the women approached and started to remember. My guide translated the tragic life stories they recounted. The little girl who stuffed two sweets into her mouth without unwrapping them had seen her mother being murdered. They'd forced the woman to bash her baby boy with a pestle, and then they'd killed her. The wary, large-eyed boy who ran away from us had lost four fingers and an ear for refusing to say where his father's friends were after soldiers killed his father in front of him. Dear Jenny, promise me that my father could never have carried out such crimes. Promise me that the FRELIMO he believed in wasn't like that. Seek him out and comfort me.

The land is almost red—it seems as if Africa is increasingly that color as the trees disappear, the war converting them into firewood, huts, food—but just above the village, the green of the vegetable garden is growing inside a fence made of booby-trapped cans to keep out the rats. The children triumphantly showed off entire collections of them, tiny, patiently flayed, ready for roasting.

I ended up finding charred remains of my father's memory. Somebody brought me a wrinkled old man, his body tough and skinny as a scarecrow, who stared at the photo a long time, filled with emotion. "Xavier. That's Xavier Sandramo." He'd been my father's neighbor and, later, his comrade in arms. To my surprise, I didn't cry. He pulled my face close to his and inspected my small eyes, very black and round, my snub nose, my round cheeks, as if he were once more looking at Xavier Sandramo. Night had fallen by the time we said good-bye. Ernesto slowly opened his arms so I could hug him, and told me, "You can breathe easy, sweetheart. Your father died a great man. Great. Like Mozambique."

Now, ever since that transformative trip, my work has been focused on Maputo: I design and redesign buildings to be simultaneously cheap, functional, and cheerful. In short, I try to pull off miracles. Which shouldn't be impossible, actually: this country's very existence seems like a miracle. They've put me up in the amazing Polana Hotel, a white colonial mansion from the 1920s with gardens, a swimming pool, an ocean view, and all the luxuries you could want. An island of privilege in the midst of destitution. At first I felt out of place in this hermetic atmosphere of diplomats and well-heeled South Africans. And then, two weeks ago, I met a woman who could be Marguerite Yourcenar's twin sister. The same wide, stubborn mouth; the same sturdy, thick body; even the same habit of twisting the family rings on her plump fingers. And most of all, the novelist's same eagle eyes. Her name is Helena Somerset, and she's a physician of about sixty who came here to teach a few classes on family planning. She saw me sitting by myself on the hotel terrace, smoking and watching the tourists, and probably thought I was depressed. She sat down near me, smiled, and said, "Amazing. I asked an employee to bring me an herbal tea because I'm not feeling well, and you know what he said? 'What you really need, madam, is a big bouquet of roses.' That's what they call natural chivalry, wouldn't you say?"

We stayed there chatting for the rest of the afternoon. Helena had married young to a wealthy English gentleman who'd settled in Porto. They had a daughter, who died at sixteen from an unidentified but devastating illness. "I don't have any family. When I go back, there's just emptiness. A huge void gradually yawned open." She says this in a subdued tone, like someone who's simply reporting on a natural phenomenon. There's no trace of the typical Portuguese "woe is me" attitude; her intense blue eyes draw a fierce line of light across her heavy eyelids, torn by a persistently defiant smile. As if she were able to view herself from the outside and be calmly astonished by the rising tide of her solitude. First her parents had died during the war, quite young, when she was just six or seven years old. Then the aunt who raised her died. Her only daughter died. And finally, her obstinately unfaithful husband took off, leaving her only that literary English last name.

She never divorced. "He asked me if I intended to remarry, and I said no, let's just let things be." She later realized she was doing him a favor by refusing to divorce. This became clear when, in the late 1980s, she went to visit him in the hospital and found him at death's door. At his bedside was a woman in a shawl and bun who begged her, "Please give him a divorce so I can marry him. I've devoted my whole life to him and I'm going to end up with nothing." Helena's reply was brief and pointed: "Marriage isn't a salaried position. You should have thought of that earlier." She turned to the patient and added, in English, "James, you should thank me for protecting you all these years."

And there she is, smiling as she enters the hotel bar where I'm writing this letter, carrying a bag full of souvenir handicrafts. In the gentle voice of those who cultivate the virtue of minimal amazement, she tells me how the face of the old man who sold her a pair of sandals lit up at the almost scandalous whiteness of her foot: "He put his black, black hands on my foot, practically in shock. It's these little moments that lend life a bit of sensuality."

Manuel Almada would have been very fond of this Helena who eases my days. If it's not a problem, Jenny, I may even send our friend Manuel this letter. I've been thinking about him a lot, but I think I can only write to him through you. You were always my guardian angel—that must be the reason. A discreet, omnipresent angel who specialized in sensitive souls with a skeptical bent, like mine and Manuel's. Souls battered by melancholy, which draws a trail of fog over the earth from which the silver of dreams continually rains down. But Helena and Manuel have already, through melancholy, reached an infinite plane where nostalgia and the worship of ruins reflect a greater wisdom, which is to seek amusement in everything—even in pain, which teaches us to laugh at ourselves. I try to shift onto that plane, but I still stumble into the crowded cannibalism of memory: I live off of the sweet taste that the dead leave on my body. A great flavor. Like Mozambique.

Missing you so much, your
Natália

10

Lisbon, October 15, 1994

Dear Jenny,

When I came back, Chess House was dying. In our family we preserve signs, phrases, the faintest ghost of a gesture for an entire lifetime, but we abandon anything tangible that's been built. Ever since your death my mother had been saying she'd think about the house's fate "someday." Finally, she'd gotten it into her head to sell it. Camila used to believe that your life with Grandpa Pedro and Tó Zé was a marvelous love triangle with you as its vertex. Since Grandpa Pedro had officially had a room of his own, she thought you'd gone back and forth between your two husbands' chambers. It never occurred to her that the primary romance in that house had taken place between the two men, and though you insist in your diary that the house was overflowing with love, my mother weeps fiercely at never having guessed what was, for her, "Jenny's secret sorrow."

I confess I am comforted by the novel sight of tears on my mother's face. I'd never seen her cry, and that absence of tears weighed on me like a private affront. I think my mother's tears come not from a posthumous communion with your supposed unhappiness, Jenny, but from a childish disappointment: that of your romance with Grandpa Pedro. Imagining you and him in each other's arms helped her see you as a real mother. Over and over she says, "How could my father have been so cruel?" and claims the house is cursed. I remember your unwavering smile, Jenny, and I know that not everything you say in the diary is true. For me there's not a whiff of the indecency that seems to shake my mother so deeply. I tell her, "Love isn't something you can judge. Love has no exterior." I make sweeping declarations of this sort, which surprise even me with their unexpected transparency. It seems that you've dropped anchor over my heart for good, that you've selected it to serve as the sound box for your soul.

My mother thinks of herself as agnostic, but she actually has a God inside her who cannot be measured in human terms. A Judaic, sometimes mocking God who exchanged the fertility of self-redeeming sins for an all-incinerating irony. A hermetic God, too pure to throw down a cross on which we might ascend to the heavens. That's why nothing I say to her ever changes her views. But at least she did agree not to sell the house. Yes, I had to threaten to barricade myself in here if she went ahead with it. But it worked.

My friends came to help me clean and organize the rooms. The spider webs were woven into thick tapestries and everything lay under a monochrome layer of dust. Certain areas seemed to have been closed off and forgotten for many years, Jenny, starting with your room. After Tó Zé died and Grandpa Pedro left, you moved into their room, but I don't think you attempted to preserve anything. Dry rot was starting to eat at the imposing—and infinitely lonely—four-poster bed. I carefully washed every garment in your trunk of theater costumes. I want to bring back the tradition of evening salons at your house, Jenny. Before moving here I'd talked about remodeling the whole house—yes, don't laugh—to make it more "functional," as I used to tell you. But as soon as I arrived I realized I couldn't do that. It would mean taking the house away from you, from Grandpa Pedro, from Tó Zé, even from Manuel Almada.

Manuel Almada helped me move in—it was with him that I opened these doors that had been closed so long. He looked forlornly at the dusty furniture, opened the piano, played the opening chords of Schubert's "Ave Maria," and told me, "Don't change a thing, Natália. Not a single wall, not a single table. Please don't change a thing." I can't remember Manuel Almada ever asking me for anything, Jenny. Almost embarrassed, I hastily replied that the house didn't deserve to be subjected to the insult of plastic surgery. Manuel laughed, hugged and kissed me, and said in relief, "The girl's a real architect after all. I used to worry that the times would turn you into just another superfluous rearranger of superfluities."

Well, I'll have to change some things. The plumbing, for example, is corroded. And many of the walls need to be replastered at the very least. Your bathroom, Jenny, has exposed electrical wires—it's terrifying. I don't know how you didn't end up getting electrocuted. In the last few years you didn't allow anyone into the house to repair anything. You said if the walls were painted, António would no longer recognize the house and would stop talking to you. He must have been the one who protected you.

But what I want to tell you, Jenny, is that, as of yesterday, your house once more contains a male presence. After my divorce I used to spend entire nights looking for Álvaro—or, rather, I tried to make him run into me in places I knew he frequented. I never found him. I concentrated hard, tried to muster that premonition that had once gripped me. When it didn't, I ended up deciding, quite reasonably, that it wasn't meant to be. I became obsessed with my father's image and seized the first opportunity to go to Mozambique. I actually found Álvaro when I came back, as I was leaving the airport. I was so startled that I ran toward him, crying, "You came to get me!" But he hadn't. He was there waiting for a girlfriend— "a friend of mine," he called her—who was arriving from Canada. "From Canada," I said, overstepping. "But Canada is a place where nothing ever happens." And I started walking, mechanically, without saying good-bye. And it was perfect timing, too, because my mother showed up a couple of minutes later—and she really had come to get me.

I hid myself away at the beach, in my work, in alcohol on Lisbon nights as the summer drew to a close. At the beginning of autumn I decided to move to Chess House. I could no longer bear the melancholy of the house I'd shared with Rui. I ended up living there alone much longer than I lived there with him, even when we were married, but his presence floated through the space like a steady ballast of well-being. In your house I buried myself in your papers, dresses, and memories, Jenny; weeded the garden; hired a couple of gardeners to prune the marvelous chessboard of your love. But when I ran out of such tasks, I knew I couldn't keep running away from myself. So I bought a rose and placed it in a transparent box with a cupid and a silver shoe that had adorned my wedding cake. And I sent the box, with a little card, to Álvaro. On the card I wrote a sentence taken from your diary, Jenny.

I know you'll understand. I even felt as if it was your hands guiding me in composing a card that would scandalize my mother. That pink porcelain cupid's destiny wasn't just to top the cake for a broken marriage. Or maybe it was; I ran across the cupid while going through drawers of keepsakes and didn't fight the urge to send it to Álvaro.

I don't want to marry him, Jenny. With him I discovered the lover's privilege of remaining alone. However much events might suggest otherwise, the women in our family don't tend toward fatalism. By your early twenties you already knew that love is a parasite of indifference, a virus that spreads in the absence of social norms and sexual practices. Your solar voice now tells me that being loved is a hassle, the complete opposite of the complacent pleasure indicated by the verb *to love*. Every experience of love has the melancholy flavor of a simulation. Maybe love is a third entity that interposes itself between two people, eliciting in them desires for perfection that are incompatible with the consummation that defines humanity. In the end I realized that it's not Álvaro or myself that I feel sorry for; I mourn the supernatural exile of that third entity, rotating in the void of a too-high sky.

I sent the box with the flower in the morning. As night fell I lit the fireplace in the living room. I'd really missed that fire. During the last few years you'd started using a space heater near your feet, and it was so sad. You steadfastly refused to light a fire, saying you were afraid an ember might leap out while you were asleep, and that firewood only made a mess. I lit the torches in the garden and out to the gate. The torches were the ones that used to illuminate your garden parties; I found them in a corner of the shed. I left the front door open and lit the candles along the way from the front door to your room, Jenny. I put on your white nightgown with eyelet trim and slid between the sheets your grandmother tatted to celebrate your entrance into the world of real love. What I wrote on the card were your words: "Come on and enter me, don't be afraid." And he did, Jenny.

About the Author

Photo © Alfredo Cunha

Born in 1962, Inês Pedrosa earned a degree in communication sciences from the Universidade Nova de Lisboa before working in the press, on radio, and on television, earning several journalism awards. She was director of the Casa Fernando Pessoa museum from 2008 to 2014. Her weekly column in the Portuguese national newspaper *Expresso* was awarded the 2007 Prize for Parity for Citizenship and Gender Equality. She currently contributes to two culture-focused radio shows and a public television show, and also works as a literary translator, notably of the work of Milan Kundera. In 2017, she founded her own publishing house, Sibila. Pedrosa has published twenty-four books, including the prize-winning novels *In Your Hands* (winner of the 1997 Prémio Máxima de Literatura in Portugal), *Eternity and Desire* (finalist for the 2009 Portugal Telecom Award and the 2010 Prémio Correntes d'Escritas), and *The Intimates* (winner of the 2012 Prémio Máxima de Literatura). Her work has been published in Brazil, Spain, Italy, Croatia, and Germany. *In Your Hands* is her English-language debut.

About the Translator

Photo © Karla Rosenberg

Andrea Rosenberg is a translator from Spanish and Portuguese. Her full-length translations include Tomás González's *The Storm* (Archipelago Books 2018), Aura Xilonen's *The Gringo Champion* (Europa Editions 2017), Juan Gómez Bárcena's *The Sky over Lima* (Houghton Mifflin 2016), and David Jiménez's *Children of the Monsoon* (Autumn Hill Books 2014). She holds an MFA in literary translation and an MA in Spanish from the University of Iowa, and she has been the recipient of awards and grants from the Fulbright Program, the American Literary Translators Association, and the Banff International Literary Translation Centre.